BAD TO THE BONE

Sated by their meal and relaxed with each other, Sherissa and Peter were quiet on the drive to Roxbury and her condo. Peter felt that so far the evening had been a success. They had explored each other's background and felt comfortable with the resulting disclosures. Sherissa had even declared that she saw Peter's work as a noble profession. That insight coming from her pleased him. *What a woman,* he thought.

Driving through the night in Peter's car, Sherissa wondered to herself how the night would end. She and Peter had talked tonight as if they had known each other for years. The conversation flowed freely and easily between them, with Peter enjoying her stories of growing up with a twin brother.

"I think most of the time," she had said, laughing at the memory, "Todd thought *he* was my parent, always looking out for me, protecting me . . . too much of *that,* really."

Sitting in the darkened car she sensed she had reached a crossroad in her life. She made up her mind just as Peter pulled the car up to her condo.

"Would you like to come in for more coffee?"

"That would be very nice," Peter answered.

They walked up the sidewalk to the front steps and Sherissa handed Peter her key. He opened the door and they each entered the vestibule. Peter closed the door and they went up to the second floor to Sherissa's condo. Each knew their relationship had moved to a new level with Sherissa's invitation and Peter's acceptance.

BOOK YOUR PLACE ON OUR WEBSITE AND MAKE THE ARABESQUE ROMANCE CONNECTION!

We've created a customized website just for our very special Arabesque readers, where you can get the inside scoop on everything that's going on with Arabesque romance novels.

When you come online, you'll have the exciting opportunity to:

- View covers of upcoming books

- Learn about our future publishing schedule (listed by publication month and author)

- Find out when your favorite authors will be visiting a city near you

- Search for and order backlist books

- Check out author bios and background information

- Send e-mail to your favorite authors

- Join us in weekly chats with authors, readers and other guests

- Get writing guidelines

- AND MUCH MORE!

Visit our website at
http://www.arabesquebooks.com

BAD TO
THE BONE

Mildred Riley

BET Publications, LLC
http://www.bet.com
http://www.arabesquebooks.com

ACKNOWLEDGMENTS

I would like to thank Tim O'Brien and Bill Roorbach, writers of extraordinary skill and talent who encouraged me to try to write. In addition I owe much to the staff and instructors of the Cape Cod Writers' Conference who guided and nurtured me. I would have been dismally lost without the support and guidance of Karen Thomas, senior editor and Chandra Taylor, editorial consultant of Arabesque BET Books. I would be remiss if I did not acknowledge the 'hand-holding' I have received from my sisterhood of authors, Rochelle Alers, Sandra Kitt and Shirley Hailstock to name only a few of those who aided, comforted and urged me to write. I cannot name all of you, but I want to thank all of you. My late husband always said you were the "cream of the crop," and as usual, he was right.

Mildred Riley
Whitman, Massachusetts

Prologue

Augustus Bell Hodges, known to associates as Mr. A.B., was almost always referred to by friends as Gus. On a recent summer evening he looked around his oak paneled office with great satisfaction. Imagine a poor, barefoot kid from a tiny, remote Caribbean island comfortably at ease in one of Chicago's high-rise offices. *Not bad,* he thought. *Not bad at all.*

Protecting his silk imported tie with his left hand to prevent it from being snagged by the desk drawer, he reached inside with his right hand to extract a Cuban cigar from a flat cigar box.

From his vest pocket he retrieved a tiny silver pocket knife, flicked it open with his thumb nail, carefully slicing off the tip of the cigar, slowly moistened it with his tongue, finally lighting it with a silver monogrammed lighter.

He leaned back in his desk chair to look up at the well-groomed, well-dressed young man who stood by, having just been called into the office.

"So," Augustus Bell Hodges said as he blew thick white circles of cigar smoke into the air, "our friend in Boston has not kept to his end of our agreement, eh?"

His speech pattern revealed many of the shadings and distinctions of the typical West Indian accent. He squinted through the smoke at his aide.

"What do *you* think, Ty?" he asked.

Tyree Embrey raised his shoulders in a noncommittal shrug, hardly causing a wrinkle in his elegant Armani suit that accented the definitive lines of his slender, strong, masculine body.

"Guess he got to be reminded 'bout his responsibility. Gone past the due date," he added quietly.

His boss nodded in agreement. Finally, evidently having made a decision, he placed his cigar in a large round glass ash tray. He reached for a manila folder.

Tyree watched his boss very carefully, knowing that the fairly obese middle-aged man whose skin was the color of mahogany, whose stone-black eyes under shaggy brows never missed anything, and whose well-manicured fingers were busily searching the folder was at this moment quietly angry. The man was very serious about his affairs. Tyree knew full well how serious he was, particularly where money, *his* money, was involved.

When he spoke again, his voice was steely, low and deliberate.

"Mr. Davona, like everyone else that deals with me, gets only *one* chance."

He found the document he wanted and looked up at Tyree, who knew instinctively that he was about to receive some important instructions.

"Mr. Davona is going to learn what it means to be into me for five-hundred thousand. His fiancée is Sherissa Holland. Her father went to one of those Ivy League schools, owns a computer chip business, got in on the ground floor, doin' well. Sherissa does some kinda morning TV show."

His cold dark eyes, fixed on his subordinate's face, never faltered as he made his pronouncement.

"Call Boston. Make sure the girl's last television

show is on Friday. Of *this* week!" he announced. "You got that?"

Tyree nodded silently and left the room.

In a small alcove adjacent to his boss's office, he picked up a phone.

"Tyree here." He continued to forward the message. "Right, Friday morning," he repeated. "She gets to the studio about four A.M. The boss wants it done then. Any questions?"

His voice was as matter-of-fact as if he were ordering pizza from a local pizza shop. Whoever was on the other end must have acknowledged the assignment with few remarks or questions because Tyree hung up, and returned to the oak paneled office to report to Mr. A.B.

He found the man who had given him the orders sitting in front of his computer. His pudgy fingers flew over the keyboard as he viewed the material he had been searching for.

"I intend to own *BAD:* the franchises in San Francisco, Houston and D.C. Great way to take care of our money situation, don't you know."

Tyree knew a comment was not expected from him, so as usual he remained silent. Mr. A.B. continued.

"I'm expecting funds from Switzerland today. Want to get my money back here in the United States. Don't want to have to be holed up in the Caribbean to spend it, know what I mean?"

"Know exactly. You want to live here in the states."

"You got that right. But Jack Davona's trouble is he believes he can be a black Ted Turner or Rupert Murdock . . . some kind of black entrepreneur with a magazine, book, or some other media enterprise."

"Think that's what he wants to do?"

"Believe so. Thinks he can do better than the fellow who started *Jet* and *Ebony.*"

"How'd this Davona guy get started, anyway?" Tyree asked.

"Got money from friends, family . . . understand his folks took out a second mortgage to help him get started."

"But then he had to come to you because he's short . . . needs more money."

"Evidently never figured on rising costs, price of paper going up, circulation going down, advertisers not always signing on."

"So how did he get in touch with you?"

"*He* didn't, but one of my friends from Vegas owes me. Told him only way to pay me back was to keep his eyes and ears open whenever opportunity knocked. You just talked to him a few minutes ago. I'm certain we will have an excellent response from Mr. Jack Davona in a few days."

One

For Nate Gamble, his rigorous training schedule was vital, and a snowy early March morning was no exception to maintaining his routine. He pulled on a sweatsuit, kissed his sleeping wife goodbye and jogged into the early wintery morning. At four-thirty the city's streetlights glowed ghost-like through the light snowflakes shrouding the gray morning. The serene quiet that muffled his footfalls pleased him. Fewer distractions made it easier for him to concentrate and focus on the strength he needed for his upcoming fight.

The fight was only a month away and Nate's long-time friend and trainer, Hector Ransom, had already told him that the intensive training regime should taper off during the next few weeks.

"Over-trainin' kin be bad, like unda-trainin'," he warned. "Muscles git too tight an' reflexes git slow. Good boxer gotta have quick reflexes."

"Whatever you say, you the man," Nate told him.

"Right. Now, afta you done runnin', drop by the gym. Got tapes of Luis Alvarez wan' you to see."

Luis Alvarez was the current holder of the welterweight title and it was Nate's goal to win the championship in the upcoming bout.

Nate's morning run took him down a back street

that opened onto the large parking lot of one of Boston's major television stations. He noticed that it was already about one-third full of cars, utility trucks, and camera vans. Some of the windows on the upper floors were lighted—early morning newscasts, Nate guessed. He looked up at the satellite dishes that hovered over the rooftop of the three-story building like openhanded supplicants reaching toward the heavens for the fulfillment of hopes, dreams, and any other favors that might be granted. Looking up as he ran by, Nate threw his own hopes for the title skyward as well.

"Made good time this mornin'," Hector commented as Nate came into the gym. His face was flushed and wet with perspiration from his ten-mile run through the city streets, but his breathing was even and regular.

"Didn' do bad at all," his trainer commented, checking his watch. "Ten miles in little over an hour. Not bad at all."

"Feel good, too," Nate added as he moved toward the locker room, peeling off his sweatshirt. A slick sheen of sweat delineated firm upper body muscles beneath his smooth, swarthy skin like a sculptor's model of a well-developed masculine torso.

"Coffee's hot when you finish your shower, and I got the tape ready."

"Okay, be a minute."

"Well, what am I up against?" Nate asked Hector a few minutes later as he reached for the mug of hot coffee his trainer had placed on the table beside the couch. His dark curly hair, still damp from the shower, smelled faintly aromatic from the pomade he'd applied to tame the wayward strands.

He sipped the coffee.

"Ahh, tastes good."

Hector pointed to a tall glass. "Have some orange juice, too. Know you're real dry after your run. Now," he turned on the couch to face Nate, "I've gone over the tape, want you to notice what Luis does with his left hand when he throws a right. 'Steada bringin' it up to make a left jab, keeps it down by his left side. It's like he puts so much into that right, forgets he's got two hands! Don't know why his trainer didn't make him change. Bad habit, mon, bad habit."

"See what you mean," Nate said after he and Hector had reviewed the tape several times.

"Now, kid, I know you got the skills to beat this dude. Believe in yourself, remember that the judges look for good, clean punches. So when Alvarez comes at you with that right, slip back and counter with *your* right on his left side. Got that?"

"Got it," Nate said.

"There's somethin' else, too." Hector's voice lowered to a conspiratorial level. "He ain't had a fight in eight months! Tha's a long time for a champion. He's bound to have plenty of ring rust."

"Think I heard that 'bout him, Hector."

"Right, but you ain't goin' take no chances!" Hector pointed at the television. "Notha thing. Didja see how he lowers his left shoulder. Tha's more space for you to get your right uppercut to his jaw!"

Nate nodded. He had seen the way Alvarez seemed to turn his left shoulder almost into his opponent. "Run that by me again, Hector."

"Sure thing, kid, sure thing."

Both men watched the tape very carefully and Hector explained in detail to Nate how he could use the knowledge to his advantage.

"Now," he instructed Nate, "tomorrow be your last ten-mile run. Train in the gym here on in 'til fight night."

He removed the rewound tape from the tape recorder and handed it to Nate. "You kin drop this off tomorrow at the TV station. Promised the sports editor I'd have it back to him before the end of the week. Says there's a slot in the door where you can drop it in."

"I'll find it," Nate told him.

Friday morning turned out to be gloomy, with a dark, drizzly rain, but it was on the warm side and Nate didn't mind the weather. His run was uneventful and he had worked up a considerable sweat by the time he reached the television station. He was glad to get rid of the bulky tape in his fanny pack because it had bumped up and down against his body with each stride he had taken, distracting him.

He retrieved the tape from his waist, still jogging as he did so. He reached the front door and jogged into the lobby. He did not see anyone around, although there were several lights on in the empty lobby. Still keeping time, he slid the tape into the designated slot, ran out of the building, down the front steps, across the sidewalk, zipping the fanny pack closed as he moved. In the gray morning rain he stepped into the street, unaware of a dark vehicle moving toward him.

Sherissa Holland had just parked her car in the parking lot opposite the television station's main building. As a mobile reporter, she was allowed that privilege so that if the occasion arose, she could leave quickly to chase down a breaking news story.

With one foot in the street, she was about to move across when she saw a dark vehicle move slowly down the street toward her. Suddenly it accelerated, hitting something with a terrifying thud. When she saw a man's body fly upward and lay motionless, her screams split the air. The car, with no lights on, sped away.

Later that morning, when questioned by the police investigating the accident, Sherissa admitted reluctantly that although she saw the vehicle moving slowly toward her from her right, its tinted windows prevented her from seeing the occupants. As a reporter, she knew how vital that information would have been.

"So, you didn't see the driver?" the older of the two officers asked. He was a heavy-set man, perhaps in his fifties, Sherissa thought, well-dressed and clean shaven. He was a light-complected man with freckles, and his manner, although businesslike, was sincere and kind. Sherissa sensed this and responded to his questions.

His younger partner, a sergeant, was also carefully groomed. He wore gray garbardine slacks and a blue blazer. His face, seamless and smooth, indicated he was much younger than the older man, who had introduced himself as Lieutenant John Williams and his partner as Sergeant Peter Linwood.

It was the sergeant who asked, "By any chance did you see the license plate number?"

Sherissa shook her head.

"Only c-o- . . . "

"C-o? That's all?" inferring by his tone that she, a reporter, should have been more observant.

"It was moving too fast for me to see the numbers," Sherissa said in defense.

"What color was it, the license plate?"

"Green and white, I think. I remember thinking New Hampshire," Sherissa said as she reached for the cup of coffee a studio staff member had brought in for her and the officers. They were not seated in the interrogation room of the police station, but rather in one of the television studio's conference rooms.

"You're a television reporter?"

Sherissa recognized the condescending tone in Sergeant Linwood's voice, the implication being, *How come you're not more observant . . . might be pretty on TV, but you're really not with it.*

The responding flush on her face embarrassed her. The lieutenant interjected in a deep, matter-of-fact voice, "Sometimes you can't believe what you have just witnessed, isn't that so, miss?"

He glared at his partner as if to say, "back off, I'm in charge here."

"Well, really," Sherissa offered, "it was raining lightly, a really misty morning, and everything happened so fast and so unexpectedly that I . . . well, guess I was. . . ."

"That's all right, Miss. You've had a severe shock. We won't take up any more of your time. We may need to question you again, however."

Sherissa nodded. "I understand. The victim, has he been identified?"

Sergeant Linwood checked his notepad. "The family has not been notified yet, so this information is strictly confidential, you understand, but the television's sports editor thinks his name is Nate Gamble."

Sherissa nodded again. She was quite put off by the handsome young officer's condescending manner. She did not like him.

He continued reading from his notes.

"He is . . . was a professional welterweight boxer. I think he was up for a shot at the championship in a couple of weeks."

He looked at the lieutenant for confirmation.

"Believe that's right. *The Boston Globe* ran a piece on the upcoming bout in one of last week's sport columns. Think it was going to be televised."

"Had a wife and young child, too," Linwood added. "Too bad," he said softly.

His remark surprised Sherissa. *So he had a heart after all.*

Two

As she sat in her tiny kitchen, sipping her morning coffee, Sherissa Holland thought about her relationship with Jack Davona. Everyone in their circle of friends agreed that Jack Davona was one of the most successful, one of the nicest men in the city. Never before had she had feelings like those she felt for Jack. He was kind, considerate, trim, athletic and very good-looking. He was focused, too. He was deeply committed to his singular enterprise, a monthly publication, *Boston After Dark*. She was not too comfortable, however, around his close associate, Leroy Hayes. She didn't know why, he'd always been pleasant, but there was an intuitive feeling on her part that made her uncomfortable.

She took a few more swallows of her now tepid coffee and pushed the cup away from her. She had to make a decision. Did she really want to marry Jack? He had asked her again last night.

"Why can't you set a date for our wedding, Sheri?" He'd held both her hands in his, waited for her answer.

"Didn't you just tell me you are going to San Francisco in a few days?"

"Yes, but that doesn't mean we can't set a wedding date. You know how much I love you . . . want to marry you. You must know what you mean to me."

"I don't mean to be so hesitant, Jack, or to put you off. It's just something in *me* that I've got to come to terms with."

"But you love me, don't you?"

"Yes, Jack, you know I do. Listen, I'll settle my inner problem while you're away, and when you come back we'll set the date."

"Promise?" He leaned forward to kiss her.

"I promise," she said to him, knowing that whenever Jack was physically close, she could not deny him. But, at this moment, as she sat alone in her kitchen, he was three thousand miles away and subtle, nagging doubts were again disturbing her.

All her life, Sherissa Holland had been secure in a special place with her family and friends. She had always received special consideration from those who loved her. She loved Jack, but she had seen how single-minded, how fanatic he was about his publication. An indistinct fear of living with a man whose fixed, deep-seated focus was on his work made her pause and wonder where she would fit into his life. She wanted to be first, but could she be? Should she be?

Six months ago she had been assigned by the station's producer to interview Jack Davona, the promising young African American who had recently launched a new magazine with a calendar of events of particular interest to the city's black urban professionals, or Buppies, as described in the local vernacular.

On the morning of the interview, Sherissa found Jack Davona's office located in the South End of the city. She was happy that she'd continued her daily running routine because she discovered that the office was on the second floor at the top of a long narrow curving stairway. Effortlessly, she ran up and followed an arrow directing her to Suite 102 at the front of the converted brownstone.

"Mr. Davona?" she inquired of the athletically built young man she spotted leaning over a broad work-table covered with news clippings, photos, and what appeared to be magazine layout material.

Jack Davona raised his head when he heard his name called, left his worktable with several quick strides, his right hand extended in a welcoming gesture.

"Miss Holland?"

"Sherissa Holland, from WHAB."

"Ah, yes, Miss Holland. Very nice to meet you."

Immediately his handshake, a firm yet gentle grasp, put her at ease. She was new in her position as a tele-vision reporter and really wanted this interview to turn out well. It was one of her first.

To her delight, her interviewee was young, not an old fogy, as she had feared, but a great-looking guy about twenty-eight years old, certainly on the young side of thirty, she thought. His skin was the color of deep rich chocolate, and his dark eyes gleamed with warmth and openness. It was a strong face she noted, with a wide smooth forehead that her father always said indicated intelligence. Jack's clean shaven face was delineated by a firm jaw line. Sherissa's pulse quickened, she felt it in her chest, so she was happy to sit down in the chair he offered. His welcoming smile made her relax a bit and she forced her mind to focus on her task. She opened her bag and took out a tape recorder.

"You don't mind?" she asked. "It helps jog my memory."

"Not at all," Jack smiled at her and she felt her ten-sion begin to subside. She so wanted a successful interview. She had to impress her producer. After all, she was the new kid on the block and the only reporter of color. She *had* to be successful.

Jack Davona found himself stunned by the attractiveness of the young woman who had just come into his office. Her skin, a creamy tanned color, was enhanced by her dark hair that she wore in a sleek no-nonsense haircut. It curled close to her cheek, and that somewhat softened what otherwise would have been a very severe hairstyle. Her eyes were dark brown, protected by thick, curly black lashes. Her black linen pants suit did little to hide her trim figure, and the candy-striped crisp cotton blouse she wore beneath the open jacket brought more intense color to her face. Jack saw Sherissa as a lovely, eager young woman. Immediately he realized he wanted to get to know her better. Before he could stop himself, he asked her, "By any chance, are you a runner?"

Sherissa looked at him, her eyebrows lifted in surprise. "As a matter of fact, I do run. And you?"

"Every morning. Unless it snows, you can find me at the Jamaica Way, running around the pond."

"I've jogged there, too."

"So there you have it," he smiled at her. "Already we have something in common."

"Not really," she countered.

"Oh? How so?" he questioned.

"I *never* run in the morning. Have to be at the television studio by four A.M. I do an early morning show."

"So you run later in the day?"

"It depends. Unless there's a news break, I'm usually free after ten, so I might run after that. Helps me unwind, clear my head."

"Know what you mean. I'm sure there's a certain amount of tension in your work. There surely is in mine," he added.

"Meeting deadlines, keeping current with what's happening . . . that's what creates my anxiety level," she offered.

"Got that right, for sure," he agreed.

"So," Sherissa began to get to her task, "I know time is valuable to you, and I appreciate you giving me this interview, so shall we begin?"

He nodded in agreement and watched as she retrieved a notepad and ball-point pen from what he thought was the largest black bag he'd ever seen. She clicked the on button of her little tape recorder and looked at him, ready to begin the interview.

Jack settled back in his chair, opened both hands in a gesture of surrender indicating he was ready for her first question. He decided he was going to enjoy himself. This young woman, Sherissa Holland, was decidedly one of the most attractive young woman he'd met in sometime. Busy as he was working on his new venture, he'd not had the time nor inclination to date. Interviewing for staff, selling advertising space, he'd been working nonstop, it seemed, day and night. This interview, this break, as it were, seemed suddenly quite welcome.

He waited for Sherissa's first question. It came.

"Why did you decide to start your publication?"

"Well," he cleared his throat, "I'm originally from Houston. Came to Boston to attend college. I majored in Business, then didn't know what type of business I really wanted to get into. However," he leaned forward, "I did notice that a lot of young blacks were new to Boston. Either had come for educational purposes or to be employed by some of the technology endeavors in and around the city."

"So what was the need for a social magazine and calendar, as you saw it?"

"Newcomers to the city needed to be able to find venues that attract them, restaurants, nightclubs, even churches that would welcome them. I also felt that social functions, a calendar of events, would be helpful, as well as other resources, doctors, lawyers, fraternities, sororities, any community or organization that a newcomer might need to establish him or herself in the city."

"And you named your publication *Boston After Dark. BAD*?"

"Yes, I wanted something that would catch the reader's attention."

"And how is *BAD* doing so far?"

He smiled. "So far, so good, I'm pleased to say. Our circulation is increasing."

"And you've been publishing for how long?"

"About a year. My staff and I decided a quarterly would be our first endeavor, and we have put out two issues this year. Have you seen a copy?" he asked. He reached into a desk drawer and slid a copy of the magazine across his desk toward her.

She reached for the slick, brightly colored magazine with a striking cover of the Boston Celtics basketball team on the cover.

She told Jack, "Yes, I've seen this issue. It's the latest one, isn't it?"

"Yes, it is. We try to feature Boston celebrities on the cover if we can."

"Do you have future plans for your magazine?" Sherissa asked.

"Indeed," Jack answered quickly. "We'd like to eventually publish the magazine in other large cities. San Francisco, New York, Washington, D.C. We believe there is a similar need for such a publication in other cities, not just Boston."

"Do you think you'll be able to do that?"

"With financial backing, yes." He hoped he sounded convincing.

The self assurance and conviction with which Jack made that statement caused Sherissa to think, *This is a man who knows what he wants and how to get it.*

She glanced around the room. Tall, slender windows, uncurtained, allowed the morning sunlight to stream into the area like an approving blessing. The large worktable, a desk and side table with a computer and printer, several chairs, all seemed to signal that this room was a place for diligent creativity. Sherissa knew she could work comfortably in such a room, sparse but functional, dedicated to work. She focused again on her own task.

"Would you mind being photographed to complete the interview . . . complete our session?" she asked Jack. "My cameraman is ready downstairs, parked in the television van. All I need to do is page him. I promise not to take up much more of your valuable time."

Jack Davona felt a quickening in his body that convinced him that he was drawn to the young reporter. It was probably her no-nonsense, matter-of-fact manner that intrigued him. He wanted to get to know her better. Much better.

"Don't think that would be a problem. Have him come right up."

After she had placed the call on her cell phone to her co-worker, Jack asked, "Do you know when this interview will be aired?"

"A week from today unless some breaking news occurs. But I can send you a copy of the tape if you'd like. Might want it for your files."

"That would be great."

He walked to the door to greet the cameraman who came in laden with camera equipment.

"You must be Miss Holland's cameraman," he said, extending his hand.

"Mark, this is Jack Davona," Sherissa said, introducing the two men.

"Mark Anderson. Pleased to meet you, Mr. Davona."

"Tell me where you want me to sit or whatever."

"I'd like a shot of you at your worktable and another at your desk with a pan shot of the magazine."

With efficient speed, Mark set up his equipment and the photo shoot was completed in a few minutes. He left soon after, telling Sherissa that he planned to return to the television station. She thanked him for his work.

Gathering up her tape recorder and notepad, she offered her hand to Jack.

"Thank you very much for your time and patience."

Jack accepted her hand and gave her a warm, friendly smile. His perfect white teeth lit up his face; that gave Sherissa an unexpected sensation in the pit of her stomach. She thought she had been straight-forward and professional throughout the whole interview session, but his next few words rattled her.

"No thanks necessary, Miss Holland," he remarked agreeably "As a matter of fact, I should be thanking *you* . . . for the publicity. Can't pay for that kind of publicity these days."

Never one to let an opportunity pass by, he pressed forward.

"I'd like to show some appreciation, however. Would you like . . . well, Spike Lee is bringing the Morehouse College Choir to Boston next week. I'd like to take you to dinner and then we can take in the concert. Let me check the date."

He reached over to a desk calendar and riffled through several pages.

"Ah, here it is. Saturday the fourteenth. Are you free that evening?" He lifted his eyebrows in question as he waited for her answer.

Sherissa sensed her own interest in becoming better acquainted with Jack Davona, but somehow, unexpectedly, a feeling of old-fashioned reserve surfaced. She usually made quick judgments. Most often correct ones, it turned out. She rarely hesitated in initiating new relationships, so what was holding her back now from accepting this very handsome man's invitation?

She didn't want to appear as indecisive as a naive teenager, and realized that he was waiting for an answer, so she nodded, saying, "I believe I'm free that night, but I have to check my calendar to be sure. Can I call you later today?"

He smiled. "Please do, and I hope your answer will be yes. I look forward to seeing you again," he said as he walked her to the door of his office, toward the narrow, curving stairway, and down to the front door of the brownstone.

"I'll be waiting for your call." Unexpectedly he leaned toward Sherissa and gave her a soft kiss on her cheek.

She ran down the brick steps to her car parked out front, the enticing, clean odor of his aftershave still clinging to her cheek.

Sherissa and Jack had continued to see each other. It had been an exciting adventure for each of them as their interest in each other grew. Boston's theater milieu could be extremely satisfying and rewarding to devoted theater patrons like Jack and Sherissa, and they took advantage of it.

Once their friends realized they were a couple, they began to be invited to many parties, as well as charity events. They attended Boston's most popular events, the *Alvin Ailey Dancers,* when they appeared in Boston, *The Nutcracker Suite,* even a production of *Ain't Misbehavin'* when it came to the city. They participated in volunteer and charity functions all over the city. For the magazine, Jack explained.

Sherissa's own career had blossomed because many of the contacts provided newsworthy items for her television show. For one of her programs she introduced a primary dancer from the Alvin Alley group and a ballerina from the Nutcracker corps de ballet that revealed contrasts and similarities for the viewers. Her producer was very pleased with the showing and the excellent rating it received.

This morning, however, as she sat at her kitchen table, she knew she was wrestling with a major problem.

Her ambivalence about marrying Jack was driving her crazy. He would be returning soon from his trip that had included unplanned trips to Houston and Washington, D.C. He called her from Washington, telling her when he expected to arrive at Logan airport.

"Can't wait to see you, Sheri. Got lots to tell you. I love you."

"I love you, too, Jack," she had responded.

When she hung up, she wondered, *Do I love you enough to take second place to your work . . . and your ambition?*

Three

Whenever Sherissa had a problem in her life, her thought was always to share it with her only sibling, her twin brother, Todd. The day before Jack's expected return, she decided to call him. When she arrived at her apartment in an older section of Roxbury, quickly dropping her bagful of groceries on the table, she went into her bedroom to the telephone.

Her home was one of the many Victorian-style homes that had been converted into condominiums. She was on the second floor. It was the first home she had purchased and she was very proud of it.

At first she had thought to talk to her brother as soon as she arrived in the apartment, but she changed her mind. She figured her anxiety at the moment would be evident, and as usual Todd would pick up, right away, on her tension like he always did and would start to lecture her.

She really didn't feel like a lecture so she backed away from the telephone and went instead to her bathroom, stripped off her pants suit, and clad only in bra and panties, reached for her favorite vividly colored silk caftan that hung on the bathroom door and slipped it over her head. Mauve, pink, white, and orange, the muted tones formed an overall geometric pattern on the sensuous softness of the sleek fabric and, as she anticipated, it soothed her tingling nerves. She felt herself relax.

She returned to her tiny, efficient kitchen and put away her purchases, a quart of fat-free milk, two packages of bread sticks, and two containers of fruit yogurt. She sorted the fresh strawberries she had purchased (she hadn't been able to resist them) and placed them in a colander that she had lined with a paper towel. But before she placed them in the refrigerator, she popped two of them in her mouth, savoring their sweet succulence. Then she poured herself a glass of milk that she carried into her bedroom and sat it down on the table beside the phone. Zeus looked up at her from his position at the foot of her bed. Stretching and yawning, the cat's sleek black fur rippled with sinewy elegance as he looked at her, his green eyes berating her with a disdainful look as if saying, *It's about time you got home.* He twitched his tail jumping off the bed and in a gesture of forgiveness, came to Sherissa and wound himself around her legs, purring in his throaty manner.

"Zeus, my man, how was *your* day?"

Sherissa ran her hand along the cat's silky smooth back and after accepting the caress for a moment, the animal moved nonchalantly toward the kitchen to investigate his dish for any treats.

"I didn't forget, Mr. Zeus," she called out after him. She had already put his favorite snacks in his bowl and smiled as she heard him devour them.

The cat had been a gift from a previous boyfriend, now long gone, but the scrawny kitten she had named Zeus had grown into a very handsome animal. She could not imagine her life without him. As proud and as haughty as he was, Zeus was always there for her. Strangely enough, he did not like Jack. Jack didn't much care for cats, and somehow Zeus knew it. Sherissa always had to isolate the cat in her bedroom whenever Jack visited. He sneezed around cats.

She was proud of her twin. Todd was over six feet tall to her five feet three, so folks found it hard to believe they were twins, often asking who was older as if they were ordinary siblings.

Todd's height advantage had enabled him to be a star basketball player both in high school and college, but although a talented and gifted forward, he was not selected by a professional team.

Delivered by Cesarean section, Todd was two minutes older than Sherissa (or Sheri, as he called her). He took his role as big brother very seriously, most often acting as if he were *years* older than she. She did allow him his protective role up to a point because although she shared her life with him, she maintained enough ego to want to do her own thing. Their parents very wisely encouraged their individuality, even though they were acutely aware of the symbiotic relationship their twins shared.

They had learned since the twins were very young that one always seemed to know what the other was thinking, when the other was upset or disturbed. Each also had the uncanny ability to sense, almost feel, the other's physical pain. When Todd had fractured his right leg in a skiing accident in Vermont, Sheri told their mother, "Todd's had an accident, I told him not to go to Vermont."

She finally dialed her brother's number in Maryland.

Her brother's deep voice boomed over the phone. "Yo! What's happenin'?"

This was the same voice Sherissa knew that manipulated, encouraged, and threatened young basketball players, many standing head and shoulders over their coach.

Having heard that voice all of her life, Sherissa was both reassured and comforted by it, and welcomed it as the familiar timbre flowed over the phone.

"Todd! You doin' okay?"

"Sure am, Sherri. How 'bout you?"

"I'm just fine. Just wanted to touch bases with you, catch up on how you're doin'. And to tell you how proud I am, we all are, of you an' your team. Goin' all the way?"

"God, kid, I don't know. If, and that's a big if, we get by St. Mary's, they're a tough team, we *might* have a chance."

"Making it to the Sweet Sixteen is nothing to sneeze at as I see it, Todd."

"You're right, Sheri, and it's the first time since I've been here at St. Monica's that we're in the NCAA basketball finals."

Sheri heard the undeniable pride in her brother's voice. She knew he had good reason to be proud of his team. St. Monica's was a small Catholic college founded by the Jesuits as a liberal arts college for African Americans. Since integration had become the law, changes in the student body, recognition of the school's proven curriculum, and a new focus had helped the college grow and prosper. It was considered one of the area's finest liberal arts colleges.

"So, Kid," Todd asked, "what's happenin'?"

"Why does something have to be happenin'?"

"Because I know you, and I know you didn't call just to chit-chat about my team, as important as that is to me, so, come on, what's your news? It's your dime, so talk!"

"Funny, Todd, how each of us knows when something important is goin' on in the other one's life, isn't it?" Sherri said.

She shifted from her chair to stretch out on her bed. It *was* her dime, her call, and Todd was her best friend besides as well as her twin. It was second nature to share her life with him.

"I've met someone," she began slowly.

"I figured that was going to happen sooner or later. Tell me about him."

So she did, and when she had finished, her brother said, "You know, Sis, that all I want is for you to be happy. Take it slow and be sure that the relationship is what *you* want. Okay?"

"Yes, Todd, I know what you're saying. I promise I won't jump into anything. Want you to meet him and soon."

"Soon as I can," he promised before hanging up. But his sister's news bothered him somehow.

Todd Holland waited until Elijah Kotambigi had folded his six-foot-ten inch body into the chair beside his desk.

"Yes, sir, Coach," the young African student said, "you wished to see me, sir?"

"Indeed," Todd said. "I have received some news this morning that I think will be of special importance to you."

"Not my family, sir?" the young man blurted out, his eyes wide with fear.

The coach raised a calming hand.

"Not your family, son, not at all. But this news will, however, affect you and your family."

"Yes?"

The coach saw the level of anxiety rise as a deepening flush began to color the young African's face, and feeling great empathy toward the young man, he gave him the news he'd received by fax that morning.

"You do know, Elijah," he prefaced his statement, "that you've been a great asset to the team here at St. Monica's. And although we weren't able to make it to the final four, it certainly was not because of you. I want you to know that I think you are the best center I have ever coached."

"Thank you, sir." Always polite and formal with authority figures, Elijah Kotambigi had not picked up many of the habits and mores of the majority of students at St. Monica's. He had been a good student with an excellent grade-point average and was ready to graduate. He once told his coach, "I must do well here. My parents wish me to go to medical school and return home as a doctor. I must go back to help my people," he said that day. His ebony face, close-cropped black hair neatly combed, and his dark sober eyes assured Todd that here was a intense, deeply focused young athlete.

Moving some papers around on his desk, Todd found the fax he'd received. He explained it to Elijah.

"This fax is from the Boston Celtics. They want you. They need a center and think you are the man for the job."

Elijah sat back in his chair, his mouth open. He stuttered, "M . . . me? The Celtics want *me?*"

"Yes, they do. As a matter of fact, they want you to fly up to Boston to discuss . . ."

"But, sir," Elijah interrupted, "I'm not wanting to play professional basketball."

"I know, Elijah, you told me before that you want to study medicine."

He leaned over, placed his hand on Elijah's knee. "Think, son, what you *could* do for your people with the millions of dollars you can earn! You could build hospitals, clinics, think about it! As a doctor you can help maybe one patient at a time. But with so much money, you can *build* hospitals and institutions that can help many."

The young man stared speechless at his coach who had just indicated that he should change his goals and plans for his future.

He shook his head, stunned by the upsetting news.

"Coach Holland, I . . . I had not dreamed of such news. I . . . I must discuss . . . "

"With your parents. I understand. By all means, you should do that. It's a very important decision for you to make and your folks should know about this offer. Can you contact them today?"

"I believe I can, sir. I have a relative who has a high-ranking position in our government. I can send a fax to him and he'll get word to my parents."

"Good," Todd said. "Now, if you decide to accept the offer, the Celtics organization will want to meet with you in Boston. I can arrange to go with you if you'd like. I have family there, my Mom and Dad, my twin sister. But first you contact your family."

"Todd!" Sherissa ran down the steps of her parents' home to fling herself into her brother's arms.

"Yo, Sis!" Todd's grin welcomed his sister as he opened his arms to her. Clasped in his arms, he swung her off her feet.

Elijah Kotambigi watched as the happy reunion between the siblings took place, mindful that it had been some time since he had seen his own family and now that he had decided to sign on with the Celtics, it could be an even longer time.

Todd turned to Elijah coming up behind him.

"Elijah! Come meet my twin sister, Sherissa. Sheri, this is Elijah Kotambigi, the Celtic's newest recruit."

Elijah bowed solemnly. "I'm honored, Miss Holland."

"It's very nice to meet you. Welcome to Boston," she said.

"Thank you, Miss. Thanks to Coach Holland. I'm very fortunate to be here."

They went inside the Holland home and it was quite evident that the elder Hollands were pleased to have their son and daughter under their roof and each reassured Elijah that he was an honored guest and welcome to visit at any time.

Mrs. Holland, the twins' mother, was a smiling, brown-skinned, middle-aged motherly type woman who looked up at the extremely tall basketball player and gestured to him to lean down so that she could give him a warm hug.

"Child," she said, "you're some kind of giant, but consider yourself another son to me. Welcome!"

Mr. Holland echoed his wife's sentiments. "Yes, Elijah, consider this your home in Boston, by all means. Gentlemen," he said to Todd and Elijah, "would you like something to drink? Come on into my den," and he led the way to a room off the living room.

A small bar with three stools was placed against the far wall. A desk with a computer and printer was situated beneath two windows with floor-to-ceiling bookshelves on either side of the windows. A leather couch, coffee table, and two smaller side chairs with a table and lamp between them made a cozy setting opposite the bar. The walls were paneled in a warm cherry wood which added to its sense of relaxed comfort.

"I know that neither of you drinks the hard stuff," he said, going behind the bar and peering into a small refrigerator. "I have all kinds of soft drinks, as well as fruit juices. Your preference, gentlemen?"

"Dad," Todd spoke up, "I'll have a ginger ale," and turning to Elijah, he asked, "Want orange juice, Elijah?"

"If you please, sir," he told his host.

Todd pulled the tab from the chilled can of ginger ale and began to tell his father about the weekend plans.

"Don't have a lot of time, Dad. Have to get Elijah here settled in at the Sheraton Hotel. But I'd like to have a quick word with Sheri, so may I leave Elijah here with you for a minute?"

"Fine, son." Mr. Holland indicated to Elijah that he should join him on the leather couch. "Those two," he shook his head, watching his son leave the room, "they may not look alike, but they are as close as can be. Tell me, what do you think of Boston with its crooked streets? They used to be cow paths, you know."

"So I've been told," Elijah said. "I'm quite accustomed to cow paths."

Todd found his sister up in her old bedroom. She was holding a pair of running shoes. She smiled when she saw him standing in the doorway.

"Like old times, eh, Todd. You coming in to check on me. How long will you be in town?"

"Just this weekend." He glanced at the running shoes in her hands. "Those your old favorites?"

"Yeah, thought I'd take them home with me. These old ones seem to fit my feet so well."

"Still running, eh?'"

"Still running. Keeps me sane."

Todd wasted no time, got right to the point. "So tell

me about your latest interest, Jack Davona, his name is? When am I going to meet him?"

"I was hoping sometime this weekend. I want you to like him, Todd. He's a terrific guy."

"Got to be if you've fallen for him."

"Think you can come by my place tomorrow night? I'll do some beans and franks," she smiled. "Boston baked beans, that is."

"And Jack Davona will be present, I take it."

"Yes, indeed. He knows I want you two to meet. And bring your Celtic with you. He might as well be introduced to Boston's traditional Saturday night meal."

Todd watched his sister search in her closet for a tote bag to put her running shoes and a pair of slim black sandals in to carry to her condo.

He was surprised that the vibrations he was receiving from Sherissa had alerted him that his twin was holding back. She wasn't as excited about this Jack Davona as she wanted her brother to believe. He reckoned he'd know for certain when he saw them together. Their interactions with one another would tell him.

Sherissa herself felt some apprehension about how Todd and Jack would react when they met each other. One thing was that they were both strong men. Would there be instant antagonism between them? she worried.

On Saturday night, when Jack arrived, Todd was quick to say, "I'll get it!"

He opened the door. "Good evening, Jack. I'm Todd Holland, Sherissa's brother."

"Hi, Todd; Jack Davona. Nice to meet you."

Todd reached for Jack's hand, fairly pulling him

across the threshold, but Jack, sensing the maneuver, stood his ground and responded with a firm grip of his own. He stepped inside as Todd closed the door behind him.

"Jack!" Sherissa accepted a hug and a kiss on her cheek from him. "You've met my brother, Todd. And this is Elijah Kotambigi, one of Todd's basketball players and the newest Boston Celtic recruit.'"

"Hi," Jack shook Elijah's hand. "How *are* you? And congratulations!"

"Thank you, sir. It's a pleasure to meet you."

"Jack, you may want to do an interview with Elijah for your magazine, *BAD, Boston After Dark,"* Sherissa suggested.

"Good idea, Sheri, a very distinct possibility."

"And how is your publication doing?" Todd asked.

Jack turned to him, still standing with a possessive arm around Sherissa. "Quite well, thank you. We did a recent article on the Celtics organization with a team photo on the cover, so an article on Elijah here would be a natural sequel, I'd say."

Sherissa could feel the tension rising as she watched Todd and Jack, each sizing up the other, looking for weaknesses and measuring strengths.

Todd observed the behavior of the tall, good-looking man whom his sister said she loved. *My sister is smart and clever, but she's not in this dude's league. He's not the one for her. No way,* he thought.

Four

Jack was sitting at his desk, willing his telephone to ring. He'd have to have some news soon. Tense and nervous, his palms were wet and the rivers of perspiration that ran down under his armpits added to his clammy discomfort. His head was pounding forcefully with each pulse beat and he wanted relief from his physical pain, as well as from his overwhelming financial problems.

On top of all that, Sheri was being difficult. She'd been complaining that they didn't spend quality time with each other anymore. She seemed envious of the time he needed to spend at the business. Couldn't she understand the stress he was under, managing to put out a publication like *BAD*—that it took every bit of attention that he could give?

Twenty-four hours a day was not nearly enough time, even with his trusted, competent staff. Why was she dragging her feet on setting a date, even though he was insistent that she do so?

"You know how busy I am, Sheri. Sometimes meetings last for hours on end. Even then I'm not always satisfied that everything is the way I want it. But I promise, soon things will ease up and you'll have me all to yourself."

"Jack, all I want is to be able to share your life, but

lately you've been so busy, we aren't doing much of that anymore, never mind setting a wedding date!" she protested.

"But, but you promised. I won't always be this busy."

"With the plan to start more publications out west and down south? Who are you kidding?"

He reached for her to kiss her. "You set the date and I'll be at the appointed place at the appointed time."

Angrily she turned away so abruptly that Jack's gesture landed on her cheek.

Acting as if he hadn't noticed the slight, his mind filled with the minutiae involved with the publication of *BAD*. Always he had to seek out new ideas, focus on what the readers wanted, how to keep the magazine fresh and exciting, how to interest advertisers, and, most important of all, how to obtain more capital. He knew that if he couldn't show that his enterprise was on solid footing and fulfilling a viable need, he would be continually struggling for money.

It was his friend, Leroy Hayes, who knew someone from Las Vegas, where he had grown up, who found a backer. If this loan came through, it would change his life.

When the telephone finally rang, he thought his heart would stop. He could hardly reach over to lift the receiver from its cradle. A second ring mobilized him.

"Davona Publications, Jack Davona speaking." His voice cracked with the tension he felt.

A man spoke, "The bread is in the oven." He said nothing more. Jack's hand trembled as he quietly lowered the receiver.

His father had warned him once, "Be careful of who you deal with. Make sure you check every angle, every possibility of what could go wrong. Understand what I'm sayin'?"

Today his father's admonition came into his mind, but as he had responded to his father that day, he remembered he had said, "But Dad, if I don't take some risks, I won't do anything worthwhile." Besides, he trusted Leroy.

The two detectives, Williams and Linwood attended the large funeral service held for the popular boxer, Nate Gamble. The lieutenant had assigned several plainclothes police officers to move about, mingle with the mourners to notice faces of persons who might seem out of place.

From their vantage point in the balcony of New Jerusalem Baptist Church, the detectives were able to get a good view of the services being held for the slain boxer.

It was a nice, clear early summer morning. The winds from the west had subsided, had chased the rain east out to the ocean. The morning sky, a brilliant blue, and the sudden surge of unexpected warm weather brought a lightness and an airiness to the otherwise somber occasion.

The church pews were filling rapidly and before long every space was filled.

"Look, Lieutenant," Peter Linwood pointed to a slight figure of a young woman seated about halfway down on the left side of the church. There was no mistaking Sherissa Holland.

"Wonder if the station assigned her to cover this . . . or did she come on her own?"

"Well, she is a reporter, and she did witness the

accident. Kinda makes for more of a connection, don't you think, sir?"

"Could be. Let's keep it in mind. Think you could arrange to catch some of her shows? You do have a VCR, don't you?"

"Oh, yeah. Comes in handy for shows I don't want to miss."

"You know, Pete, it seems unlikely that a welterweight boxer and a female television reporter would have anything in common."

"I know. One of the things they taught us in school; leave no stone unturned."

"I know, I learned that same thing early on in my career," the lieutenant agreed. "But didn't I hear that the young woman is dating the guy who publishes *BAD?* Jack Davona, I think is his name. Have you seen the magazine?"

"Yeah, I like it. Up to date, lots of pictures, some pretty good articles. And I believe I've heard they're planning to get married."

"I'll have to get a copy of the magazine, look it over."

"Got one at home. I'll bring it in," Pete whispered as they both heard the Pastor's deep voice intoning, "I am the Resurrection and the Life," as he walked slowly down the aisle in front of a bronze casket. Weeping could be heard from the deceased man's family and friends as the somber procession moved forward to the front of the church.

For the next hour the two detectives observed the rituals at the church, as well as the grave site. Sherissa Holland did not show up at the cemetery, but the lieutenant took note of two white men who remained well in the background. Probably associated with the fight game. He watched them leave in a large black limousine parked near the gate. He noted the license plate. It was a rental, but had New Hampshire plates. He jotted the number down. 460NH.

Back at the police station, John Williams poured himself a cup of coffee. He had brought a sandwich from home so he unwrapped it at his desk, and after waving an offer to share with the sergeant who declined, he began to eat.

He chewed thoughtfully for a few minutes, sipped some of his coffee and after a while, raised a finger to alert Peter, whose desk was across from his.

"We've got to get background history on the dead man, the television reporter, her boyfriend and the boxer's wife and trainer. Need a complete report on each of them. You start with the reporter and the boyfriend and I'll take the boxer's wife and trainer.

Linwood nodded in agreement. "I'll start right away." He was pleased with his assignment because he wanted to get to know more about Sherissa Holland. He'd intended to find out more about her anyway and now he had permission to do so. There was something about the young woman that made him believe she disliked him, and he wanted to remedy that if he could. Her tone of voice when she'd responded to their inquiries that first time right after the accident, the distance she kept from them, and the fact that her answers were so matter of fact. Of course Linwood could understand the trauma she felt, but he still couldn't help but feel her antagonism. The next time he interviewed the young lady, he would do his best to get by that barrier.

The lieutenant was just finishing his brief lunch when one of the desk clerks came in and handed him the medical examiner's report on Nate Gamble. The list of injuries was long, including several fractures, head injuries such as a skull fracture, many chest injuries in which several ribs had crushed the man's heart and lungs. Cause of death was "multiple fatal injuries caused by motor vehicle accident."

The lieutenant shook his head as he read the report. A well-developed, well-nourished healthy young man had been tossed about like a rag doll. Whoever hit him meant to kill him. His responsibility was to find out who did the dastardly deed . . . and why.

He decided to start with the boxer's long-time friend and trainer, Hector Ransom.

"Yes, sir, Lieutenant Williams," the trainer's voice came over the telephone. "I'll be right here at the gym."

In response to the police officer's next question, he added, "Anytime's a good time, quiet today . . . after the funeral an' all. Wanna come at four this afternoon?" His voice cracked with emotion. "Gotta fin' out what bastard offed my guy, nicest guy inna worl' . . ." the man's voice trailed off.

"We're doing out best, sir. See you at four."

Lieutenant Williams found the gym in an old part of the city. The red brick structure was close by an abandoned railroad car barn. Many railroad tracks crisscrossed the street and he drove over them very carefully.

Unexpectedly, he found the interior of the building to be bright and clean. Various boxing equipment, such as speed bags, punching bags, and exercise apparatus ringed the perimeter of the large room, in the center of which was a standard-sized boxing ring. Along the far wall were two doors, one marked Office and the other marked Locker Room. In one corner the lieutenant spotted a desk with chairs. Hector Ransom was sitting there, but the moment Williams entered he got up from the desk to great him. After they had exchanged handshakes, the trainer escorted the detective back to his desk.

"So," the police officer asked, "how long had you known Nate Gamble?"

Obviously grief stricken, the man nodded his head while trying to control his emotions. Williams waited. Finally regaining control, Hector answered huskily. "'Bout ten years."

"Ten years?"

"Yeah, 'bout that. Nate was eighteen, jes' startin' out in the business. Came into my gym here to train an' I spotted him as a guy wi' talent. When afta a few years as an amateur, he turned pro, asked me to be his trainer."

Looking at the grieving man, the detective thought that perhaps the man had been a boxer himself at one time. About fifty-five years old, he had a way of walking as if coiled like a tightly wound spring, ready to repel any physical attack that might threaten him. His bronze-toned face had been made homely by the many scars to the connective tissue over his cheeks and eyebrows. He had obviously taken many blows during his career. It was a thin face, but the trainer's eyes were straightforward and unflinching. The detective figured he could trust a man who made eye contact with him. Great sadness was apparent, as well, and the officer empathized with the trainer.

"Did you think he had the possibility to take the championship?" he asked.

"Oh, no doubt! Without a doubt." Hector responded. "Pound for pound he was the best welterweight in the business!"

"Mr. Ransom," the detective leaned forward, notebook in his left hand, his pen poised in his right, "do you have any idea who would want Nate Gamble dead?"

He waited for the man's answer, acutely aware the man was reluctant to give him an answer.

"Did he have enemies inside or outside of the ring?"

He watched as the trainer sat back in his chair, his head resting on the top, his eyes closed as if trying to summon a response. A few seconds passed before he lowered his head, opened his eyes, and answered in a soft voice.

"Been thinking 'bout that since it happen', hit an' run, you say?"

The detective nodded.

"Unnerstan' I don't really *know* anythin' . . ."

"Mr. Ransom, anything you say now will be kept in confidence, and sometimes it's just a *little* thing that can be very important in trying to solve a crime."

"I know, I know, watch them TV shows."

"Well, then, you know how valuable the slightest information can be."

"Nate was married, you know. Nice girl named Natina. We called her Tina. So the two of them wouldn't be Nate and Nate. They had a son, Nate, Jr., but they call him Trey because of three Nates, don't you know."

"Interesting." The policeman was taking notes.

"Yeah, right, but Nate was a good provider, worked at the airport, baggage handler, you know, loading luggage on the planes. He worked the three to eleven shift."

"That helped build up his upper body, I take it."

"Yeah, right," Ransom responded with his usual

phrase. "It helped. He was strong, but the best thing he had goin' for him was his speed. Hands like lightning. But . . ." he shook his head, remembering his loss, "he an' Tina were very much in love. He was crazy about her and she likewise. The only problem was there was an old boyfriend of hers who kept coming 'round, almost like stalking. Nate worried about Tina because he didn't want the guy botherin' her, especially since he worked the third shift. Told me he finally had to take out a, what you call it?"

"Restraining order."

"That's it. Now I don't know if the guy stayed away or not."

"His name? You know it?" Williams had his pen poised over his notepad.

"Alex—Alexander Brown. Guess from what I heard, he was some type of jock in high school, good athlete, but never did anything with it. Understand he hangs out at a bar down the South End. Never met the guy myself, jus' heard 'bout him."

"Well," Williams checked his watch. "I thank you for your time, Mr. Ransom."

"Oh, call me Hector, nobody calls me Mister."

"Hector, it is then," the detective smiled and extended his hand. "Please believe me when I say we'll find the person or persons responsible."

"Sure hope so," Hector added, his face wrinkled with concern. "There's another thing, too. I heard that Tina was so scared of this Alex guy stalkin' her, she carried a cell phone so she could call 911."

Five

The management of WHAB made the decision to distance itself and its reporter, Sherissa Holland from the tragic accident that cost the life of Nate Gamble. A brief news item memorialized the event as occurring in front of the station, with no mention that one of the station's reporters had witnessed the fatal accident.

The station manager explained his policy about the matter to Sherissa, "I don't want our viewers to focus on this event, or to think our station is where untoward events might take place."

"I understand," Sherissa told him.

"Right, and besides, we want to protect you as much as possible. Too much media coverage on one of our reporters would not augur well for our station."

"I do understand, sir, and I appreciate your concern."

So, in a way, she was surprised when the station's manager's secretary buzzed her to say that a Sergeant Linwood from the police wanted to interview her.

"Tell him I'll be with him in a few minutes. And Gina," she asked the secretary, "can you direct him to the conference room? I'll meet him there."

She wanted the presence of the large oak conference table and chairs to lend some formality to the interview session. From that first encounter with the young detective, she had disturbingly ambivalent feelings toward him. From the first he alienated her with his arrogance that made her feel that he thought he knew everything . . . and could almost see inside her head, read her mind. And he seemed eager to throw his weight around, as if police authority gave him permission to do so. She'd noticed how he tried to impress, to use his college education against the senior officer's up-through-the-ranks education. She wondered how Lieutenant Williams could tolerate the novice. But then she did sense the handsome young sergeant's sensitive side.

In physical appearance Peter Linwood was attractive, well-groomed, with a handsome mustache that added distinction to his smooth shaven nut brown face. She remembered him as being taller than she, probably five-ten, with a lithe, supple frame. He looked as if he took care of himself.

She hurried to the conference room, anxious to put this unexpected interview behind her. Whatever could she tell him except to repeat what she'd already said? She found the conference room door open and she spotted the detective gazing out of one of the windows that looked out over the parking lot across the street. He turned to face her as she entered, extending his hand. She shook hands with him, quite aware of a strong grip.

"I'm glad you agreed to see me on such short notice," he said, smiling at her. His smile seemed genuine and sincere and Sherissa wondered if he meant to reassure her, but her anxiety level eased immediately. Perhaps this interview would go well, she hoped.

"The department means to locate and prosecute the person or persons responsible for the death of Nate Gamble," Peter said, "and to that end I'd like to ask you a few more questions since you were a witness, the *only* witness we have."

"Be glad to tell you what I know," Sherissa said. "It was a terrible thing! I could hardly believe my eyes. All of a sudden the car appeared out of nowhere and a body was flying through the air right in front of me," she shuddered at the memory. "I'll never forget the sight and the sound of the thud when the car struck him."

"Sorry. It was awful for you, I know."

She sat down in one of the chairs across the table from the policeman and watched as he took his inevitable notepad and pen from his inside coat jacket.

He looked over at her and when he spoke, his next words nearly jarred her out of her seat.

"Miss Holland, do you know if anyone wants to kill you?"

"Kill me?" her mouth dropped open. "What are you talking about? Kill me?"

"You were the only other person on the street that morning besides the victim."

"So?" She drew a deep breath. "What's that supposed to mean?"

"Well, I understand that you jog frequently and on that day you were wearing black sweats, and as it turned out, so was the victim."

"It was a rainy, misty morning!" she insisted. "I had planned to run after my morning broadcast." She felt her face begin to flush, where had he gotten such a preposterous idea, anyway?

"How could I be mistaken for a man?" she questioned. "I'm nowhere near as tall or as big as he was."

"Your head was covered, no one could see your face?"

"Yes, I was wearing a dark rain hood, but I still can't

understand. Kill me? Sergeant Linwood, you're crazy! How can you think of such a thing?"

She jumped to her feet, glared at the man who'd dared to make such a preposterous suggestion. Her face flushed a deep red and she began to shake. She made herself walk to one of the windows, look out at the street where it seemed to her now her normal life had begun to change. What now was in her future? Who would want to kill her? She thought of Jack's many friends, some of whom she sensed moved in fast, upscale circles. At first she was excited to be a part of such high-style people but then Jack refused to sign a prenuptial agreement. He denied that their marriage could *'ever, ever'* fail. It took days to convince him to sign it just in case.

She turned from the window to return to her seat across from Peter Linwood.

He had upset her greatly by his suggestion and he knew it, but well, sometimes you have to shake the tree for the fruit to fall. He watched her. She seemed to be making a determined effort to get herself together.

"Sorry if I upset you," he said quietly. "Can we start again? You're all right?"

Sherissa nodded.

"If you would, can you tell me in your own words what you saw that morning?"

She sighed. "I had just pulled into the parking lot, got out of my car, it was raining, still fairly dark . . ."

"What time was that?" Peter Linwood interrupted. He noted that Sherissa had a habit of twisting her short hair around the back of her left ear, a gesture that he thought rather endearing, like something a young girl might do.

"It was about four-thirty. Takes me twenty minutes

to get to the station from my place. I left home ten minutes after four, as I recall."

"Okay, so you got there at four-thirty. Still rather dark."

"Right. When I saw it was raining a little harder, I pulled my hood over my head and was about to step into the street to cross . . . I was right across from the main entrance to the building, about to dash over."

"That's when you saw the car?"

"Yes. It seemed to be moving slowly, coming from the right. I waited for it to pass."

"At that time, had you seen the victim?"

"Saw . . . a man jog down the front steps. His head was down, seemed to be doing something with his belt."

"Was wearing a fanny pack," the detective said. "About the car?"

"Suddenly sped up and hit him! I couldn't yell or anything to warn him," her voice cracked with emotion as she relived the scene.

"Thanks. I believe I've got a picture of what happened. You did get the license?"

"Like I told you, only the letters C and O, and the green and white plate which made me think it was a New Hampshire license plate."

"And the car?"

"A Mercedes, I think."

"Well, thanks again for your time." He closed his notebook and stood up to leave. Sherissa stood as well, ready to leave when Peter Linwood asked her an unexpected question.

"I understand that Jack Davona is your fiancée. That right?"

"Yes it is. Why?"

"Like to talk to him sometime later."

"Why? He doesn't have anything to do . . . with anything."

"Leave no stone unturned. Police motto, don't you know," he explained. "Thanks again, Miss Holland." And he was out the door, leaving Sherissa more confused than ever. Jack was still pressing for a wedding date, and for some reason she didn't understand, she was getting cold feet. Now this—someone out to kill her?

Six

Boston's newest mayor had decided community policing would be one of the hallmarks of his tenure. To that end he had promoted the refurbishing of some police headquarters and building entirely new facilities in other areas.

The hit and run accident which killed Nate Gamble was in a precinct that had recently opened one of the new police stations.

The two-story brick building sported a facade that reminded one of a motel with ample parking spaces in back of it. There was a green lawn in a circular area with a flagstone path to the center decorated by a tall flag pole. A hedge of boxwood trimmed the edge of the center lawn.

Inside, the booking area was to the left of the marble-floored lobby and across from that area were offices for the police chief, his immediate staff, and the accounting office. A few holding cells were in the basement, along with other storage and maintenance facilities.

The patrolmen's squad rooms, a gymnasium with exercise equipment, and the detective offices were located on the second floor. Lieutenant Williams and Sergeant Linwood's desks were face to face in a corner of the squad room. This was a busy place. Telephones were ringing constantly, officers were conducting their assignments, messengers were delivering pertinent information and fax machines were spitting out sheets of factual information, needed to manage police business.

Both men were accustomed to the frenetic activity and were able to concentrate on their tasks in spite of it. If the turmoil became too hectic, they might opt to have a lunch break at the nearby delicatessen, The Good Egg, where the sandwiches were made of more than just eggs, to Peter's delight. He favored a nice ham on dark rye, with hot coffee, whereas the lieutenant preferred a bacon, lettuce, and tomato sandwich with a tall glass of iced tea.

They were discussing the information each had gathered from their interviews the day before.

"I'm not surprised that the young lady was flabbergasted when you asked her if she could have been the target," Williams remarked. "Why *did* you suggest that to her?"

"Don't really know. I'd heard that she was engaged to that guy who publishes *BAD*, you know, the magazine I told you about, and I've been hearing that he's been scoutin' around for funds, that maybe, the scuttlebutt is, he doesn't mind where the money comes from."

"That so? Well, fast money and the boxing world sometimes get in bed together."

"And," Sergeant Linwood added, "my sources indicated that *she* comes from money. Her father started the Holland Company . . . something to do with computer chips. And there's been talk of a prenuptial agreement. Seems as if her folks don't want their future son-in-law to tap into the family coffers. And when I mentioned that she might well have been the target, she got really upset. I saw horrible fear in her eyes."

"I take it you plan to interview the boyfriend?"

"As soon as he gets back in town."

"And speaking of boyfriends, seems that the dead boxer's wife has been stalked by a previous lover, one Alexander Brown, to the point of her taking out a restraining order and carrying a cell phone constantly in case she has to call 911."

"Think he tried to get rid of the boxer?" Peter asked.

"Dunno," Williams shook his head. "I intend to check him out first thing tomorrow. Then maybe I'll visit the widow, see if I can find out what's what."

Jack's plane from Washington landed at Logan Airport at eight the next evening. By the time he walked to the parking lot, paid his parking fee, and drove through the tunnel into the city, it was nearly nine. He called Sherissa on his cell phone, but there was no answer.

"Sheri," he said in his message, "I'm back home, can't wait to see you. Call me as soon as you get this message. Love ya!"

He hoped she had the answer he'd been thinking about and mentioning to her each time he'd called while away on his trip.

Do we have a date for our wedding?

It was all he could think of whenever he wasn't involved in his publishing endeavors.

As he drove to his condo in the city, his thoughts lingered around Sherissa's seeming reluctance to set a wedding date. Sometimes he could actually feel her withdrawing from him, a definite chill in their relationship. He tried to think back to what could have caused her spirit, her warm passion, to wane.

The first months of their courtship had been great—the many parties, frequent theatre outings, with Sheri always looking beautifully well-groomed and well-dressed. Jack knew there was never anything wrong with having a beautiful woman on your arm when you appeared in public. That was something Jack had learned long ago. When he arrived at his office the next morning, still perplexed because he hadn't been able to reach Sherissa, he went ahead with several staff meetings, anxious to catch up on what may have occurred during his absence. It was nearly one in the afternoon before he received her call.

"Sheri, where have you been and why haven't you returned my calls? I've been worried! You Okay?"

"I'm fine, Jack. And you, did you have a good trip?"

"Girl, you don't sound fine to me. You're not sick, are you?"

She laughed. "No, I'm not sick, but a lot's been happening since you've been away."

"The job?"

"Well, not exactly that. Listen, why don't you slide by tonight and I'll fill you in."

"Got lots to tell you, too, honey."

She heard unmistakable pride in his voice. What was he going to say when she told him about the accident and . . . that she couldn't marry him?

John Williams drained the last bit of coffee from his cup and thanked his wife.

"Good breakfast, my dear. Now you *will* be ready for tonight, won't you?"

He was rewarded by a huge grin from his wife of thirty-five years.

"With bells on, kiddo! You can believe it," Helen said.

"You know it's funny," he said as he bent over to kiss her.

She looked up at him from her seat at the dining room table, "What's funny?"

"Kendra asked me the other day what it was like to be married to one woman for thirty-five years."

"And what did you tell your daughter?" His wife tilted her head sideways as she waited for his answer.

"Told her I really wouldn't know because her mother was never the same two days running!" He laughed.

"That's the way it's supposed to be," Helen quipped. "Keeps things interesting. In a marriage, never know what's coming next."

"Gotta say you've been able to do that." He bent over to kiss her. "Honey," he said softly, "it's been great, every minute of it. See you tonight."

He backed his car out of the garage, reflecting on his good fortune. He loved his work. Sorting out and solving crimes kept his mind active. He enjoyed working with his fellow officers, even young upstart Peter Linwood, who, with his college degree, thought he knew it all. But Williams knew he'd pull him around. The kid was honest and sincere, that made for a good start. As the lieutenant drove from his home on the outskirts of the city proper, he was glad he'd been 'grandfathered'; because of his thirty years' tenure, he did not have to meet the city's new residency requirement and reside in the confines of Boston proper.

It was a beautiful spring morning. The sun had forced the forsythia to lacey yellow blooms that decorated many of his neighbors' lawns. The fresh, newly minted leaves of the trees, along with the early spring bulbs, added to his happiness. And tonight he and Helen were going to have a special anniversary dinner at the Top of the Hub, one of their favorite places where the revolving restaurant offered changing views of the city.

As he neared the city, he turned his thoughts to the case he and Linwood were trying to solve.

Who had struck down the boxer and why? Was it the wife's former lover, who seemed to be obsessed with her according to what the trainer, Hector Ransom, had said? Maybe an "If I can't have you, no one else can," type of obsession. Or could it be malevolence on the part of his erstwhile opponent, Alvarez, to somehow injure Gamble. Perhaps to cause a postponement of the championship bout?

Who else? Could the trainer himself be involved? Was he as sincere about his boxer's well-being as he seemed to be? Could he have an ulterior motive?

He wondered what his sergeant's interview had turned up. As he thought about it, it seemed funny that at a busy television studio the only two people on the street at that early morning hour were the boxer and the female television reporter. Could *she* have been the intended victim, and why? He was anxious to see what Linwood had learned.

He also had to check nearby repair shops to see if any damaged cars had been brought in, especially shops that serviced foreign makes.

Forensics had indicated that the victim's clothing had been torn, fibers from the sweat suit might be found on the fenders or bumpers of the involved car. Flecks of black paint had been found embedded in the victim's sweat suit. Find the car! A priority of the highest order, the lieutenant thought to himself.

* * *

Early summer weather can be capricious and unpredictable, and that week in June the weather in Chicago suddenly became sultry and humid. It was not at all the kind of weather Gus Hodges preferred. Hot he could endure, but not the oppressive muggy humidity. He decided to fly to New York in his private jet.

"Tyree," he told his trusted aide, "getting outta here. Tell Youngblood be ready to leave for New York in the mornin'. Got some business there. Got to leave this friggin' weather!"

After arriving in New York and satisfactorily concluding his banking business, he took Tyree along in a rented limo to Foxwoods Casino in Connecticut. "We might have some luck. You never know," he told Tyree.

Tyree did fairly well on the slot machines, but his boss did not.

"I'm goin' to turn in, Ty. No sense sending good money after bad. Your luck seems to be holdin', so good luck! See you at breakfast."

After he had showered and put on his silk pajamas, he decided a nightcap was in order. He poured himself a bit of his favorite rum, Mount Gay, from Barbados, added some fruit juice and a tad of coconut water that he'd brought along with him, sat down in the lounge chair, elevated his feet, and turned on the television set.

The local news didn't interest him, but he watched it anyway while he savored his drink. The weather here in the east was certainly more comfortable than Chicago's hot, steamy atmosphere. His banking business had gone well, and when Jack Davona got his message and began his payments, all would be well. If he continued to default . . . well, a publishing business would be as good a place as any to put his money.

He was about to push the remote to turn off the set when he decided to check the stock market report.

Along the bottom of the market coverage, headline news was shown. Gus Hodges almost dropped his drink when he read the report. *Local welterweight boxer victim of a hit and run accident in front of TV station WHAB.*

Damn, Leroy messed up. Again!

Seven

Jack had said that the earliest time he could get to Sherissa's condo would be late. "Sometime after seven, Sheri. Have a lot of loose ends to tie up. You understand how it is when you've been away from the desk," he added.

"After seven would be fine, Jack," she told him. Indeed, it would give her more time to think about how she was going to tell him that the wedding was off. Funny, now that she'd made her decision, she wanted to terminate the relationship quickly and cleanly.

Since this was not a festive occasion, she decided a simple seafood salad with crackers, coffee, and slices of pound cake would have to do. She knew she wouldn't feel like eating much, and Jack was very conscious of his weight so he wouldn't want a large meal.

A little after seven, Sherissa heard her doorbell peal. Wearing black slacks and a white shirt, she opened the door to a happy, smiling Jack who spread his arms in a wide greeting.

"Ta-dah! I'm back, baby. Come here!"

He reached for her, enveloped her in his arms and kissed her. The lack of warmth in Sherissa's response startled him and he leaned back to peer into her face.

"What's wrong? That certainly was not a welcome kiss."

"I *am* glad to see you, Jack. Come into the living room. I've got a lot to tell you. Do you want something to drink? Wine? Beer? Something stronger?"

"From the way you sound, Sheri, perhaps the 'something stronger'." He followed her into her living room.

Jack looked around. The room was the same, beige rug, floral-patterned loveseat in front of which was a glass-topped coffee table and a small black lacquer chest that Sheri used as a bar. On either side of the rose-and-tan loveseat were small Chinese decorated tables, each with gold and red enamel lamps. It had been a room where Jack had spent many happy times falling in love with Sherissa and planning their future despite Zeus's dislike for him. The cat would always raise his tail in a signal of defiance and stalk out of the room whenever Jack came around. They just didn't like each other.

She handed him a drink, his favorite, bourbon and water, then took a seat in one of the side chairs across from the love seat. The look of nervous apprehension on her face alerted Jack that he was not going to like whatever it was that she was going to tell him.

He took a sip of his drink.

"Tell me," he said quietly, his eyes never leaving Sherissa's face.

"I . . . I almost don't know where to start."

"At the beginning," he prompted.

"That's just it, I don't know when the beginning started."

"When I left," he said soberly, "it was my understanding that we were engaged and when I got back you would have set a wedding date. Start with my leaving."

She nodded her head soberly, her hands twisting in her lap.

"Right. It was a week or so after you left and you called to say that you'd taken care of your affairs, and I remember I had a dental appointment after the next day's broadcast. I rested most of the following day, letting the anesthesia wear off, had a root canal done, and the day after I went to the station at my regular time. It was a dreary dark mornin'one I'll never forget." She shuddered visibly. The anxiety that clouded her face warned Jack. Sherissa Holland could never have been viewed as a shrinking violet type, at least not to him. Looking at her now, nervous, on the verge of panic, instinctively he knew her news was going to disturb him.

"I know as a television reporter I'm supposed to be able to view terrible things and report on them. But this?" She shuddered. "I guess it was because it was so unexpected. Out of nowhere it seemed . . . suddenly this black Mercedes comes out of the darkness, hits and kills someone right in front of me!"

She covered her face with both hands, shook her head as if to shut out the horrible memory.

"My God, girl! What an awful thing!" He put his glass down on the coffee table, walked over to Sherissa, took her hands to sit beside her on the love seat.

"Honey, I'm so sorry! Why didn't you call me about it? I'd have come back on the red eye, you know that."

"I know, but what could you have done?"

"Been here to support you."

"You had your own agenda, and I didn't want to interfere with your schedule."

"I take it the police are investigating. Who was the victim, by the way?"

"A boxer named Nate Gamble."

"I've heard of him. As a matter of fact," Jack said as

he reached for his glass, "we had planned to do a piece on him, one of Boston's up and coming black professional athletes."

"Perhaps you can still do the article if the police find out who hit him. You know, they have already interviewed me—twice!"

"Why you?"

"Because I was the only witness. And just yesterday the sergeant assigned to the case suggested that perhaps someone was trying to kill me!"

Jack's face turned dark with fury. He slammed his glass down on the table, reaching for her. "Are they crazy? How can they think something like that?" But deep in his mind he realized that the benefactor that Leroy had connected him with would kill, even an innocent person, to get what he wanted.

"Something about my being out on the street at such an early hour. That maybe I was the target."

"You're just a television reporter, for God's sake," Jack fumed. Then he must have realized that he had misspoken. He hastily added, "I don't mean that like it sounds, honey. You're a gifted reporter or you wouldn't have your job, but to kill you? Now, this boxer, you've never interviewed him for television, have you?"

"Never. But, Jack, they know that you and I have been close and they want to talk with you, too."

"Any time," Jack said, "Any time. I've got nothing to hide." He hoped he sounded convincing. How could he give up *BAD*?

He tried to sound positive but he felt a gut-wrenching churning deep inside his body. The police couldn't know about the 'bread in the oven'. Or could they?

He reached for Sherissa. "Look, honey, we can't

let this sidetrack us, upset our plans for our future. You know how much I love you and want to marry you."

Sherissa drew back from him and he was attempting to keep her close when her response came.

"We *can't* go on . . . be married with this investigation over our heads," she said.

"Of course we can! This situation is unfortunate, but has not one damn thing to do with us, with our lives!" Jack insisted.

"It does. Already the station manager has asked me to distance myself. He does not want the television station too closely involved with the whole situation. As he said to me, 'We don't want to be identified as the TV station where bad things happen.' And, Jack, somehow the police know that we have already signed a prenuptial agreement.

"So what?" he said angrily. "What business is it of theirs? I don't believe this! The police are interfering in our lives. I'm going to put a stop to this. I'm determined to get back what we had. They have no right to take our lives from us because they can't solve a hit and run case. Don't know who they're messin' with, but when *Boston After Dark* gets through with them, they'll know!"

He stormed out shortly afterwards, too frightened and too upset to eat the meal she had prepared.

After he left, promising that nothing was going to come between them, Sherissa fixed a small plate of food for herself, took it to her room, and sat at her desk. Zeus looked at her from his favorite spot at the foot of her bed, stretched and yawned, as if to say, *One more hurdle over.*

Sherissa responded to the cat's unspoken remark,

saying, "Wonder why Jack got so mad when I mentioned the prenup?"

The cat nestled his head into his curled body as if to say, *Beats me,* and went back to sleep.

Eight

"So," Linwood asked his superior officer, "how did the anniversary celebration turn out? Have a good time? The missus was pleased?"

"Couldn't have been nicer," Lieutenant Williams told him. "Thanks for asking. We had quite a time, quite a time," he reflected. "You got a steady girl-friend, Sarge?"

"Not at the moment. Just got through a long-term relationship that fell apart, so I'm cooling it for now."

"Well, let me tell you, son, there's nothing in this world like the love and support of a good woman."

"So I've heard," Peter said as a quick flash of the lovely Sherissa Holland flickered into his mind. He wondered how she was doing and reminded himself he still had to interview the boyfriend, Jack Davona. The guy should be back in town by now. He made a mental note to check on the publisher's whereabouts. Like he'd told Sherissa before, always have to turn over that last stone. Never know what lies beneath it.

"You know," the lieutenant looked across his desk at Peter, "that Hector guy has got a prior."

"Really?"

"Yup. Actually, Ransom is an alias. Real name is Frank Nicholas. Seems he was picked up as a mule down in Houston. Did time there for being a middle-man in drug trafficking."

"Houston? Isn't that where that Davona guy is from?"

"Believe so, Pete. Think maybe there's a connection between the two? When you interview the publisher, try to see if there is some relationship, okay?"

"Sure, Lieutenant, will do."

"Good. Now let me fill you in on my Ransom interview. Couple of things came to light. One, he'd been the boxer's manager for sometime. The kid was quite good, tried out for the Olympics, showed a lot of promise. Anyway, Hector Ransom, a.k.a. Frank Nicholas, picked him up, got him to turn pro, and brought him along to this . . . . a chance to go for the welterweight championship. Not sure yet how much money he'd have gotten if the kid had won the crown."

"Could have been quite a bundle."

"That's what I think. Probably should have asked. Anyway, he's devastated that Gamble got himself killed. But he told me something else, too."

"Another lead?"

"Right. I started to tell you about it yesterday. Seems as if Mrs. Gamble was having trouble with an ex-boyfriend. According to Ransom, he was obsessed with her, so much so that she finally took out a re-straining order to keep him away from her. And she carries a cell phone with her all the time so she can call 911 in case he continues to stalk her."

"He could have a motive for killing her husband," Peter said.

"I'm checking him out today."

"He have a rap sheet?"

"'Couple of prior arrests. DUI, had his driver's

license revoked. Have to find out where he was at four-thirty the morning of the accident. Now, fill me in on the details of your interview with the television reporter, Sherissa Holland."

"She didn't have much more to tell than what she'd said when we interviewed her right after the accident. Of course, she was quite shaken up at the time, but the facts remain the same. But . . ."

The change in the sergeant's voice alerted Lieutenant Williams, and he gave full attention to Peter's next words.

". . . one interesting thing she didn't tell me . . . I got the info from a lawyer friend . . . she and her fiance have signed a prenuptial agreement."

"Really?"

"Seems it was instigated by her folks. They have plenty of money. Her old man is president and CEO of some computer business, makes computer chips or something. They seem to have their doubts about their prospective son-in-law."

"But I'm sure it takes a lot of money to publish a magazine. Where did he get his money to even start up?"

Peter shook his head. "Maybe I'll be able to find out when I get to interview him. I expect to catch up with him soon. He's been out of town awhile. Sir," he asked, "have the boys been able to find the car?"

"Not so far. Going to ask if we can extend our search to Brockton, Fall River, New Bedford. Maybe even out of state, Rhode Island and Connecticut. Could be whoever killed Gamble had outside connections."

"Wouldn't be surprised," Peter agreed.

* * *

The lieutenant had no difficulty locating Alexander Brown. Because of gentrification, many upscale restaurants, art galleries, gift shops, and trendy clothing shops had sprung up in the South End, catering to the tastes of the wealthy urbanites who had relocated there. However, there still remained remnants of the once vibrant black community. One of the oldest was a restaurant with a bar that served soul food and kept the brothers and sisters that frequented the place happy with the Friday and Saturday night jazz venues offered. For many years since the end of World War II, Zachary's Place was the trusted, beloved haunt of the community. Patrons had always been drawn by good jazz, fine food, excellent liquor, and warm camaraderie.

The fresh spring air outside was invigorating to John Williams after leaving the stuffy, closed-in squad room. He walked to his unmarked car, a rather beat-up Toyota, to drive to the South End. He thought about his destination, Zachary's Place, and remembered his first visit.

He had promised his father that he wouldn't smoke or drink until he was twenty-one. So, on his twenty-first birthday, his father took him to Zachary's Place.

"Now that you're considered to be a man," his father said, "I want the privilege of buying you your first drink."

He gave John a hearty slap on the back. "You've been a good kid and I'm proud to be your dad."

John often remembered that special day with his now deceased father, and that afternoon when he entered Zachary's, warm memories of that eventful day filled his mind. The expansive feeling of becoming an adult, being on a level equal to his father, returned full force when he stepped into the place.

At this hour of the day Zachary's was quiet. The 'going home' regulars who usually stopped by for a quick drink had not yet arrived and the few late lunch goers were leaving; mainly senior citizens who had not only eaten their barbequed chicken, greens, sweet potatoes, and cornbread, but were able to take home leftovers for their evening snack.

There were tables along two walls at right angles to each other. A moderately sized dance floor in the center, with the bar on the far wall. Service rooms and the kitchen were behind the inside wall. Several older men were at the bar. John guessed they had been nursing their drinks along most of the afternoon, but would be leaving as soon as the paying customers came in. Living on fixed incomes, they knew they had to allow the bartender to serve the customers who had money to spend.

John recognized the bartender, a man about seventy years old, pushing a damp cloth over the oak bar.

"Afternoon, Mr. Jones."

"Well, Lieutenant Williams, long time no see!" The man's grin was a welcome one.

Albert Jones was a tall, thin man with a slender caramel-colored face. Dark brown eyes beneath thick eyebrows as white as his hair made him look as if he'd seen all types of adversity, but had survived.

"And how are you, Mr. Jones. And the missus?"

At the detective's innocent inquiry, the man's face clouded over.

"My wife passed away 'bout two months ago."

Williams reached across the bar to shake the man's hands.

"Mr. Jones, I'm sorry. I didn't know. Mrs. Jones was such a lovely woman. Please accept my heartfelt condolences."

"Thank you, son. We almost made it to our fiftieth wedding anniversary, but it wasn't to be, I reckon," he said.

John Williams recalled the happiness he'd experienced only a few days before when he and Helen celebrated their thirty-fifth wedding anniversary.

"I'm very sorry. Again, my deepest sympathy to you and your family."

Mr. Jones cleared his throat, removed some glasses left by the customers and turned back to the police officer.

"So, do you want something to drink, or are you here in an official capacity?"

"Oh no, sir, nothing to drink. I'm here looking for someone that I'm told comes in here frequently. A guy named Alexander Brown."

"What's old Alex done now?"

"Well, that's what I don't know. His name came up in an investigation I'm doing and I need to talk with him. Is he here?"

"Not at the moment. Comes in about this time of day usually . . . if he comes."

"Know where he lives?" Williams took out his notepad.

"Believe he rents a room over on Springfield Street."

"Does he work?" Williams asked Mr. Jones.

The bartender wrinkled his forehead in thought for a minute, then said, "I'm not sure, but seems to me I heard something about him working at that big storage facility."

"The one that looks like a fortress, you mean?"

"That's the one, Lieutenant. Wait a minute, let me check." He beckoned to a young man who had just taken a stool at the end of the bar.

"Jonathan?"

"Yes, Mr. Jones?" the customer answered.

"Don't Alex Brown work over at that storage place on the avenue?"

"Last time I heard he was there. Just saw him a few minutes ago talkin' to some friend down the street. Told me he'd see me in here."

"Thanks," He looked at Williams for a response.

"Mr. Jones. I think I'll wait for a while. If Alexander Brown does come in, can you point him out to me, and do you have a place where I can talk to him privately?"

"Of course, right in my little office," he pointed to a door at the end of the bar.

"Thanks. Thanks a lot."

Nine

"Friday, the twenty-eighth?" Alex Brown asked. "To answer your questions, Lieutenant Williams, I wasn't in town. No way could I be in no accident. Don't have a license, anyhow." Confidence oozed from the suspect's voice.

John Williams was no stranger to fast-talking suspects like Alexander Brown, who fit the typical profile of Boston's borderline citizenry.

Dark skinned, with jet black eyes, Alex was a healthy, well-built, well-nourished, well-dressed young man. The lieutenant thought, *Probably he has more female admirers than he knows what to do with, but from all accounts, he is fixated, obsessed with another man's wife.*

"You're not the first person to drive a car without a license," Williams reminded Brown, whom he noticed made steady eye contact, as if refusing to back down. The policeman continued with his questions.

"Out of town, you say?"

Brown nodded.

"And you can prove it?"

"Sure can." The young man pulled his wallet from his back pocket, searched through its contents, pulled out a ticket stub which he handed to the policeman.

"Went to the opening game of the Red Sox in New York. See, here's my ticket stub."

"So you left Boston at four A.M.?"

"At four A.M. on the twenty-eighth I was down at Park Street station to get the four-thirty bus to New York City."

"Why so early? The game starts at one in the afternoon and it only takes about four and a half to five hours to get to New York City."

"Bunch of us got a special deal by leaving at that time."

"Well, I'll need to speak to someone who can verify that you were on that bus, at that time, on that day. The ticket stub is not enough. Could have picked that up anywhere."

"Went to New York, I tell you! Nothin' to do with no hit and run accident!"

"But you were interested in the dead man's wife, weren't you? Could be a motive."

"I'm over *that,* man!" Brown exploded. "Over that! Got me a foxy chick now, a nurse at Mass General. Just about engaged. No time for Tina Gamble!"

As Lieutenant Williams told Peter Linwood about the interview when they met the next morning to compare notes, Alexander Brown was not clever enough to make up an alibi, so he probably was out of town as he said. "Did give me the name and phone number of his alibi witness and it seems to check out. He did go to the Red Sox opener. How did you fare with the magazine publisher? Catch up with him?" he asked.

"Lieutenant, that man is an operator."

"Tell me what you discovered."

"Well, for one thing he's looking for money."

"Money?"

"For more money. I guess he had enough seed money to start up his . . . his publication, but apparently costs are going up and the advertisers have slowed down."

"So you think he may be running short."

"I gather that's why he's been flyin' all over the country."

"Hmmm. I wonder," the lieutenant said, "how he could be tied up in this hit and run."

"Lieutenant, I have to tell you something else that struck me funny."

"What's that, Pete?"

"He was hotter than a firecracker when I went to his office."

"Mad?"

"Mad! When his secretary ushered me into his office he jumped up like he was ready to hit me. His face was blue-black with rage and his eyes were like black stones, staring at me. He was mad! 'What business do you have questioning *me*?' he roared at me. Of course I stood my ground, knowing that I had the policeman's badge, which I flashed at him right away seeing as how I was in plain clothes. I told him, 'This is a routine inquiry and I am gathering evidence and would appreciate your cooperation in the matter.'"

"So did he? Cooperate, that is?"

"Quieted down a bit after blustering and boasting that he had friends in high places and he intended to complain about police harassment."

"How did you get him to calm down?"

"Told him that I was making a routine inquiry, gathering evidence, that sort of thing, but that if he'd rather, we could continue the interview at precinct headquarters."

"And that did the trick?" John asked.

"Right. He was fairly cooperative after that. Perhaps

I'm wrong, but somehow I sensed he might be involved in that vehicular homicide."

"If he was as mad as you said he was when you approached him, could be because he has something to hide," John suggested. He went on to add, "I do have a bit of information about the car, Pete. Seems that the car that struck Gamble down was a Mercedes."

"That was Sherissa Holland's guess. How do you know for sure?" Peter wanted to know.

John Williams leaned toward his desk and tapped a large brown envelope laying there.

"I was sitting here thinking about the case, about the victim, about how badly injured he was, and I figured forensics had photos of the body, so I called and asked for them. I knew they would keep them for evidence."

He crooked his finger at Peter, beckoning him to view the photographs he had shaken out of the envelope. He pushed a few of them around. Peter saw black and white pictures of a nude male body badly traumatized. The pictures had been taken from various angles and some were close-ups of specific areas. He winced when he saw the horrible pictures of a battered male body.

John handed his sergeant a magnifying glass. "Look at that bruised spot on the victim's lower back, just below the kidney area, and tell me what you see."

Peter Linwood was glad that the photographs were black and white and not full color because he was still uncomfortable around dead bodies, but he looked closely at the area the lieutenant indicated. He realized he *had* to—part of the job.

"Looks almost like he was branded. A triangle inside a circle."

"You do know, Pete, that the boxer's clothing was

badly torn and almost ripped from his body by the force of being struck. Know what I think made that dark bruise?"

Peter shook his head.

"That triangle and circle is the hood ornament of a Mercedes Benz. That's what I think made that bruise. The victim was hit so hard his body was flung up on the car's hood, landing him on his back on top of the ornament before his body flew over the car and onto the street."

"So," Peter surmised, "we know a Mercedes could have been involved. And we've got a partial identification of the license plate."

"I'm running this info through DMV, the Registry of Motor Vehicles, right now and we'll see what comes through."

"John," Peter said thoughtfully, "Jack Davona drives a Mercedes."

"I know," the lieutenant said softly. "The license plate tag is C-O-B-A-D. It's a Massachusetts plate framed by a green plastic holder."

"But he was out of town! We know that."

"Someone else was driving the car."

"But who? Any why?"

"Son," the lieutenant said, replacing the photographs back in the brown envelope, "that's what we're going to find out."

Ten

When leaving the television station, Sherissa unexpectedly ran into Lewis Osgood, the station manager. She met him at the front door as he was coming in to work.

"Oh, Miss Holland, how is the police investigation going? Heard anything?"

"Good morning, Mr. Osgood," Sherissa responded to the middle-aged man who held the door open for her.

"I haven't heard anything more about the accident. The police . . ."

"Still investigating, I presume," he interrupted.

"I . . . I believe so."

"Well, a horrible tragedy," he conceded. "Have a good day, Miss Holland," he said as he moved forward into the building.

"Thanks," Sherissa murmured as she made her way down the front steps. She couldn't help but wonder if the 'tragedy,' as Mr. Osgood put it, would effect her life more than it already had.

She was glad that she had plans for the evening. Elise Daniels, one of the secretaries at the station, had become a good friend and had suggested that they attend a networking event to be held that night at a local hotel.

"Never know, girl, who you might run into." She was aware of Sherissa's breakup with Jack. "Take me, for example," she said to a reluctant Sherissa. "I've been ready to scout the field since I dumped the last sorry brother who was wasting my time!"

Sherissa nodded her head at her friend.

"Know just what you mean," she said, thinking about her failed relationship with Jack, who was continually calling her, leaving messages on her answering machine. She wondered if she would have to resort to a restraining order. Should she check with the police? Seeing Mr. Osgood reminded her of the incident, and Peter Linwood came to mind when she thought about police protection. She began to wonder about the case and . . . had Peter interviewed Jack as he proposed to do? What was the outcome?

She picked Elise up at the front of Elise's parents' house. Bright and bubbly, Elise drew people to her with her outgoing personality.

Sherissa watched her rush down the front steps, her short, natural haircut framed her cherubic, round face. Elise made Sherissa smile as she bounced breathlessly into the passenger seat of Sherissa's car.

"Looking good, sister-girl." Sherissa admired her friend's outfit.

"Been dyin' to wear it," Elise told her. "Still can't beat Filene's for their basement prices. Only paid twenty-nine dollars for this pants suit."

"I love that soft green color. Goes well with your skin tone," Sherissa said as she drove away from the front of the house, down the street. "What kind of material is that, anyway?" She touched the sleeve of Elise's outfit.

"They call it pseudo suede. 'Sposed to look like suede, but I think it's some kind of synthetic stuff."

"Well, you'll be a hit. The brothers will be all over you, girl"

"Think so, do you?" Elise shot back. "Don't look too shabby yourself!"

"I didn't know *what* to wear," Sherissa confessed as she negotiated a turn onto the main highway. "Went to the closet and grabbed the first thing I laid my eyes on. Always figure you can't go wrong with black," she said, referring to the black faille suit she was wearing.

"Right about that."

"Elise, I hope I'll meet someone interesting."

"Oh, me too!"

"I don't mean someone to get involved with," she hastened to add. "I mean someone interesting for my television program. My producer is always looking for, as she puts it, 'new faces and fresh ideas.' It wouldn't hurt my standing at the station if I could produce some new and innovative people."

"You do what you have to do," Elise said. "Me, I'm lookin' for romance. A 'Mr. Right', if you know what I mean. Sheri, girl, he's got to be out there, somewhere! I just have to *find* him."

"Well, you go, girl, and good luck!"

A few minuts later Sherissa drove into the hotel's parking lot and began to look for a parking spot.

"Elise, from the looks of these cars around, these could be some eligible males. Never saw so many BMWs and Mercedes. Look, there's even a Jag! Course," Sherissa said, "could be owned by sisters, as well."

"Know what you mean!" Elise checked her makeup in the mirror behind the sun visor. "Make ways, boys, here I come, ready or not!" she mocked cheerfully.

Sherissa laughed, realizing that she needed the loose, carefree feeling that Elise offered. She'd been too tense these past few weeks and it was a relief to let go for a change.

There were groups of people in the hotel lobby. Some seemed to be heading to the conference room on the second floor while others seemed to be waiting for friends to join them.

Sherissa and Elise took the escalator to the upper floor to the room that had been designated for the workshop. They registered at the table just inside the door, then found their way to a table where they discovered other people from Station WHAB.

Mark Anderson, Sherissa's favorite cameraman, offered to order drinks.

Sherissa accepted, saying, "You know what I'd like, Mark."

He gave her a wide grin, responded quickly. "One Fuzzy Navel comin' up!"

"Make that two, please," Elise added.

"Done and done!" Mark quipped as he hurried to the bar.

"I don't believe it," Sherissa said.

"Don't believe what?"

"The young man standing over there. He's wearing a slate gray suit."

"You mean that *fine* young brother talkin' with that older woman? You know *him?*" Elise asked.

"I don't *know* him, but I do know who he is."

"So?" Elise wanted to know, her curiosity aroused.

Sherissa obliged her. "That's the policeman that came to question me at the television station."

"That's him? I didn't recognize him. I remember now, I saw him in the conference room the day he came to interview you."

Sherissa shivered as she remembered the horrifying feeling she'd experienced when Peter Linwood told her she might have been a possible target for a murder. She still couldn't believe such a possibility existed. Why? She didn't have any enemies. Not that she knew about, at any rate. She forced her thoughts back to the occasion at hand and took a sip of the drink in front of her. She raised the glass in front of Mark. "Thanks again," she said, and he acknowledged her gesture with a smile. "Anytime, Sheri, anytime."

A young man moved to a podium in the front of the room to make an announcement.

"Good evening all and welcome to our first minority workshop. My name is Steven Ames, your host for tonight. We want you to mingle, move about, get to know one another, exchange business cards. And to that end, a buffet table has been set up at the table to my right. Mingle and enjoy. And if we succeed tonight, we may do this again."

There was an enthusiastic applause from the participants and many began to move in the direction of the food table.

Mark asked Elise and Sherissa if they wanted him to get food for them.

"No, thanks," Elise responded promptly, "think *I'll* look over the *brothers* while I check out *the food.*"

Sherissa said, "No, thanks, Mark. You go on ahead. I'll get something later."

She watched as both Mark and Elise left the table, chatting with each other and new acquaintances as they neared the buffet table.

She felt quite alone. Usually at functions like this Jack Davona was at her side, catering to her every wish. But now, with her broken engagement, those days were over. She thought to herself how unmoved Todd was when she told him.

"I knew he wasn't right for you, Sheri, the first time

I met him. Not for *my* sister," he added. "He was very impressive, very smart, but something about his persona, an aura about him, that I knew you would not have been able to live with. Physically, a very attractive man, but morally and mentally . . . I would always have had reservations."

Lost in her thoughts, Sherissa was not aware of someone standing close behind her chair until a deep, husky voice made her look up into the face of Peter Linwood.

"How nice to see you again, Miss Holland."

"Sergeant Linwood."

Sherissa hoped that her mixed emotions on seeing the policeman didn't register on her face as she indicated to him to have a seat. She really hadn't sorted out her feelings . . . didn't truly know how she felt about him. She realized she didn't care too much for Peter Linwood the policeman, but how about Peter Linwood the man? How did she really feel about him? Tonight he was very attractive in his elegant suit, silk tie, and well-polished tassel loafers. She decided tonight to respond to Peter Linwood the man.

"It's nice to see you. Not here on police business, are you?" she asked.

He laughed heartily.

"Ah, no, not tonight, Miss Holland. Not officially, at any rate, but a police officer is always on duty, so to speak. No," he added as if to allay her fears, "friends of mine from out of town insisted that I come with them. They needed directions, anyway, so I decided I'd shepherd them here tonight. You know how intimidating Boston's streets can be. So, now, meeting you here, I'm glad I came."

Eleven

"Don't bother taking off your jacket," Lieutenant Williams said to Peter. "Just got a call from Chief of Detectives, a homicide at the park. Fill you in on the way. Let's go!"

Peter did as he was told, grabbed his cell phone from his desk where he had just deposited it, and clattered down the stairs to the parking lot where he joined the lieutenant who was already in the car and had started the motor.

"Who got it this time?"

"Dunno, Pete. Chief said 'Get right over to Franklin Park, dead body on the golf course.'" The lieutenant drove out of the police station's parking lot, making a quick left turn toward the public park.

"Jogger found him 'bout six-thirty this morning," he explained to Peter as he negotiated through the morning traffic.

When the two men arrived at the scene, they walked quickly to the area cordoned off by yellow police tape.

Williams spoke to the police officer in charge. "What've we got?"

"Name is Leroy Hayes. Found a driver's license in his pants pocket. DOB 5/5/65, makes him thirty-seven, I think."

"Medical examiner notified?" the lieutenant asked.

"Be here in ten minutes," he said.

"Good. Well, Peter, let's go have a look at the victim."

Not at all anxious to see a dead body, Peter moved slowly across a green fairway toward a thicket of large shrubbery forming its edge. Nervously, he plucked at the senior officer's elbow—both to gain his attention, as well as slow down the pace of reaching the body.

"Lieutenant, er, John, did Moxley back there say the guy's name was Leroy Hayes?"

"Yeah, right. Know him?"

"Don't think so, but I've heard the name before somewhere."

"Rings a bell with you, eh? Sometimes the best clues come to you that way. Believe it or not, son, it's not always a scientific problem. Sometimes it's intuition or common sense that provides the answers."

"Realize that," Peter admitted.

He bent down closer to get a better look at the body. It all seemed so incongruous to him; a lovely, enticing, clear summer morning and a victim whose morning ended in death. Shivering with distaste as he neared the victim, he saw the body of a man lying in a crumpled position as if tossed from a vehicle to the ground. The man appeared to be about five-feet-ten-inches tall, perhaps one hundred fifty pounds. He was light-skinned, with close cropped black hair, and wore a well-groomed mustache. He was dressed in dark cotton shorts, a red Harvard sweatshirt, and white sneakers.

Waiting for the arrival of the medical examiner before they touched the body, Peter remarked to the lieutenant who was walking around the area, "Suppose he was running?"

"Could be," Williams answered. "I see there's an access road right up on that slight rise." He pointed to a dirt road about twenty-feet from where the body lay at the foot of the small hill.

"We're going to take a look around, Officer," he said to the young policeman. "Let us know when the M.E. gets here. Want to check that road."

He and Peter scrambled to the top of the well-manicured lawn to the road.

"Look," the lieutenant pointed.

"I see them," Peter answered.

Definitive tire tracks were clearly visible in the reddish brown soil. They were double striations grooved into the soil with a well-marked pattern as if a vehicle had remained in position for a few minutes.

John Williams pointed this out to Peter. "See, up ahead, where they took off in a hurry. Stopped long enough to toss the body out, then hit the dirt. You can see the skid marks. Moxley," he called down to the policeman, "have forensics get casts made of these tire marks and cordon off this area, right away! No traffic in or out!"

"Right, sir. The M.E.'s here."

"Coming! Come on, Pete, let's see what the doctor can tell us."

As they moved down to the murder scene, John Williams, in a soft voice, chided his inexperienced assistant. "I know how it feels when you first start out in this homicide business, Pete. What you have to do is put your own feelings aside."

"You're right. It's just getting used . . ."

"You never do get used to it, son. What you do have to remember is that the victim was somebody loved by a mother, father, sister or brother, has been fatally harmed, and it's our responsibility to find that person or persons who did it and bring them to justice. It's not a nice job, I know, but look at it this way, it's a job vital to maintaining law and order in a civilized society."

"You're right, John. Learned that in our criminal justice classes. But I gotta be honest, I've learned a whole lot more these past few months working with you. I mean that. Books and learning procedures are one thing," he gave his partner a side-long glance as they reached the car and he opened the door on the passenger side. "There's no deal like the real deal, that's for sure."

"You're learning, Pete. You'll do just fine," John reassured him.

"So, what've we got, Doc?" John Williams asked the medical examiner, a youngish-looking black man who wore horn-rimmed glasses now perched on the top of his forehead.

His serious look when he stood up from a kneeling position beside the corpse alerted the two police detectives that they had another murder on their hands.

"A single forty-five to the back of the head did your victim in, but there could be other injuries, too. Will know more after I've completed the post."

"No sign of a gun or shells nearby?" John asked.

"Didn't see any when I turned the body over."

"Can my men take him away now, Doctor?"

"Certainly, detective," the doctor said as he stripped off his rubber gloves and closed his medical bag with a sharp snap.

"Dr. Burton, I don't believe you've met my new sergeant detective, Peter Linwood."

The two men exchanged handshakes.

"My pleasure, Dr. Burton," Peter said, happy to note that the young doctor's hand was warm and firm, not cold and clammy like he thought it might be since the doctor dealt with death. Ashamed of himself for his inappropriate thought, he responded to the doctor with a firm handshake.

"So, your previous partner . . . ?"

"Retired," John answered. "Gone to Florida, tired of our fickle Boston weather."

"I understand perfectly. Took some time for a lad like me from Barbados to get accustomed to the kind of climate you folks have up here."

"Doc, know when you'll be able to do the post?" the lieutenant wanted to know.

"As soon as I can. Have a couple of cases to finish up first, but hopefully by late afternoon."

"That will be fine. Okay guys," he called to the police officers waiting for his directives, "M.E.'s finished. Take him away." Then he turned to Peter, "There goes Leroy Hayes. Now we have to find out all we can about him. How and why he died."

Several criminologists were methodically searching the area where the body had lain. Blood samples soaked into the ground from the head wound were collected. Peter spotted some coins in the area. He pointed them out to John who was wearing rubber gloves. The silver quarter and two dimes were placed into a plastic bag.

"Not sure if we can get prints from these, but you never know."

"We going back to the station now?"

"Right, Peter. Don't think we need to stay." He gave a few more orders to the police remaining at the scene, then he and Peter walked back to their police cruiser.

"John," Peter said thoughtfully, "I think I've seen or heard that guy's name before, like I told you. Wish I could remember, but it will come to me."

* * *

"Of course, be delighted to rent my first floor apartment to a police officer," Mrs. Wallace said to Peter when he had asked about her first floor vacancy.

"My late tenant, Mr. Snell, was a security guard for close to thirty years down at Symphony Hall, so it's almost like carryin' on a tradition, isn't it?" she smiled. "Happy to have a law man around."

Now Peter let himself into his first floor apartment, anxious to shower and change to remove the aura of death that seemed to cling to him. He wondered, *Would he ever become accustomed to dealing with death as part of his work as a homicide detective?* He rounded up his mail from the hall floor where it had fallen from the mail slot in the front door. He didn't bother to even glance at it, his mind focused on getting rid of the disturbing feeling he had.

A quick invigorating shower, a change into comfortable sweats refreshed him. He grabbed a bottle of beer from the refrigerator, sat down in his big lounge chair and with the remote in hand flicked on the television set. It did not take long for him to realize that there was nothing on the tube that interested him. He took several swallows of his cold beer, then rested his head back on the chair. He closed his eyes and immediately Sherissa's lovely face surfaced in his mind. He thought about the conversation he'd shared with her at the networking event. The black faille suit she wore was in such elegant good taste, understated by the white silk blouse with a soft bow at her neckline. Small gold hoops swung from her earlobes whenever she turned her head. Peter was entranced by her fragile beauty, but he realized, too, that this girl maintained an inner strength that one might not recognize at first.

He had asked her, "Do you come to events like this very often?"

"No," she said, shaking her head, making her gold earrings flash. "This is my first, and I came with one of my friends."

"You're not looking for a new job?"

"No," she broke in, "just a chance to see new faces. Everything is grist for the mill, you know, and I'm always on the lookout for interesting personalities for my television show."

He looked around the room. "I know what you mean. Never know who you may run into at a gathering like this."

"Always the policeman, right?"

"Well, you never know." He hesitated for a moment as if reluctant to reveal what was on his mind. "Look, Miss Holland," he stuttered, "I . . . I'm afraid I've gotten off on the wrong foot with you."

Sensing his discomfort, she said, "How come?"

She saw the apologetic half grin that came over his face as she waited for him to explain.

"Well, I had the feeling that when we first met I somehow came off to you as an egotistical cop who figured that he knew it all. But I want you to know I'm really not like that at all. As a matter of fact," he continued, "I'm not sure of very much except that I've got a lot to learn . . . things they never taught in college."

"I expect on-the-job training is really where it's at. I know I've learned more about television since I've been in the field."

"So," Peter leaned closer to her, "can we start off again tonight on more even footing?" He raised his eyebrows in question, giving her a tentative smile as if hoping for a positive response.

Sherissa smiled back at him, impulsively offered her

hand, which he shook enthusiastically. "Of course," she said. "By the way, I suspect you can't reveal much, but are you making any headway on the hit and run case?"

Soberly, Peter confessed, "You're right, I can't talk about it. But, yes, we have uncovered some leads."

"Sure hope you can find out who did it."

"Doing our best, Sherissa." Then he added, "Is it all right to call you Sherissa?"

She smiled broadly at him, sensing suddenly that she wanted to know him better. "If I can call you Peter, Sherissa is just fine."

He reached for her hand again, saying, "Before your friends come back to the table, I want to give you my card. If you *ever* want or need to get in touch with me, I want you to be able to do just that."

She took the business card he offered her, noting the seal of the City of Boston on it, and slipped it into her purse.

"Don't forget, *anytime,*" he urged.

He stood up when Elise and Mark returned, relinquishing his seat to Elise. "So nice to have met you both," he said, shaking hands with Mark and nodding to Elise. "I'll get back to my friends," he explained. "They're from out of town, don't want them to think I've forgotten them."

When he left he didn't hear Elise's remark to Sherissa, "Girl, he's *fine!* Definitely a keeper," she raved.

Sherissa shrugged her shoulders. "He's okay, I guess."

"Okay? Girl, don't let him get away! He's *more* than okay. Now that you're free, you'd better snatch him while the snatchin's good."

She shook her head again, admiring the strong, stalwart moves of the man who walked away.

As he sat in his living room that evening running the scene over in his mind, he wondered, did he have a *chance?* Would he be able to pursue a relationship with Sherissa Holland after this investigation was over?

He sat up in his chair, reached for the bottle of beer and saw the pile of mail he had not looked at. Several bills, he saw, and another credit card offer. Quickly he tossed that aside. *Newsweek* and a copy of *BAD* were left.

He picked up the magazine, noting that it had been produced in a format similar to *EBONY* magazine. It was the same size as *EBONY* or *LIFE* magazines, with the title in large red block letters on a black background in the upper left-hand corner at the top. A sidebar featured some of the pertinent articles covered inside the publication.

Peter noted that the major part of the cover showed a picture of Denzel Washington who had recently been given a special honor in Boston. That event was elaborated upon in the magazine. In addition, the sidebar invited readers to check out a new restaurant serving Caribbean food, and there was a reference to some recent recruits trying out for the New England Patriots football team.

Peter riffled idly through the pages, looking for the article on the well-known actor, Denzel Washington. As he returned to the front of the magazine, searching for the contents to find the page of the Washington article, he noted the editorial page that listed the publisher and owner, Jack Davona. But beneath that name another name fairly leaped out at him: Leroy Hayes. Wasn't that the name of the victim of this morning's homicide? Peter reached for the telephone.

Twelve

"You know, Pete, what you told me last night when you called started me thinking."

"Yes, sir. About what?"

Lieutenant Williams went over to the coffee pot on a nearby table. It was kept hot most of the day like an eternal flame. He poured himself a steaming cup of black coffee. Peter declined a refill of his own cup, anxious to hear what John had to say.

The lieutenant took a tentative sip of the hot brew before he answered.

"After we left the scene, Officer Moxley got a plaster cast of the tire tracks we saw yesterday. They were made by a fairly new Mercedes, one with a special, distinctive tread. Now we already know that it was a Mercedes that hit the boxer. Could the same car be involved in this case? And now you say the victim, Leroy Hayes, is Chief of the editorial staff of Davona's magazine, *BAD*?"

"Think there could be a connection?"

"I do, Pete, I do. Sometimes it's just fragments of threads, pieces of information that can be put together to form a picture or a series of events that may lead us to our target."

He took another satisfying sip of his coffee before placing the cup on his desk. He raised both hands, joined steeple-like in front of his face, rested his chin on his hands. Across the desk from him Peter Linwood tapped a pencil on his desk. The older man saw the sergeant's forehead crease into frowns.

"Something on your mind, kid?"

Peter nodded. When he spoke, his voice was low and somber.

"Have to confess . . . I was fresh and facetious when I interviewed Miss Holland . . ."

"How so?"

"Well, thought I . . . to tell you the truth, I don't know what I thought. She is a very attractive young woman and I guess I wanted to impress her with my police knowledge and so-called smarts, and why I suggested it, I'll never know, but I asked her if she could have been the target of the hit and run."

"And she said?"

"Told me I was crazy. Who would want to kill her?"

"Don't be upset that you suggested that to her. Always have to look at all angles in a criminal case. But you know, Pete, I'm wondering if there *is* a connection between Davona and the two victims. Could it be that the girl *was* the intended victim? She was engaged to be married to Davona, wasn't she?"

"Understand she broke it off, but he is still pursuing her, finding it hard to take no for an answer. I expect you're going to be upset with me, but I *did* give her my card . . . in case she remembered something or needed, you know, police assistance of any kind," Peter confessed.

His superior officer nodded his head. There was calm understanding in his voice when he replied, "No harm, unless you make your relationship with Miss Holland more than a professional one. She is an appealing, attractive young woman, but keep your distance, at least until our work is finished. I know you understand."

"I do, and I intend to keep it that way."

Until the case is over, he thought to himself.

The two policemen went down to the South End to Jack Davona's office. The young secretary tried to stop them from going into Jack's office.

"You need an appointment to see Mr. Davona," she protested, but backed away from her boss' office door very quickly when Lieutenant Williams flashed his badge.

"Don't need an appointment. We're here on police business," the lieutenant stated calmly as he and Peter strode into the surprised magazine publisher's office.

"Hey! Hey! What's all this? Who are you?" He stood up quickly from behind his desk, glared at the police who had walked unceremoniously into his office.

"I am Lieutenant Williams, and this is Sergeant Linwood."

"Yes, yes, I recognize him! He's already interviewed me. What is it now, more interviews?" he said, sarcasm evident in his voice.

"Not at the moment, sir," John Williams said quietly. "I believe a member of your staff is Leroy Hayes?"

"Yes, Leroy is chief of my editorial staff. What about him?"

"Sorry to have to tell you, but he's been in an accident."

At this news, all color drained from Jack's face and he slumped into the chair behind his desk.

"Is, is he in the hospital?"

"Afraid not, sir. He's dead."

"Dead?" his voice cracked as he repeated *dead*. "He

can't be! He left last night on a seven-thirty flight to Las Vegas. He was in yesterday morning, but his father was in the hospital, heart attack. He was flying out to be with him. Are you *sure* that it's Leroy?"

"We identified him by his license we found in his pocket. Of course someone will have to make a positive identification . . . perhaps you?"

"No, no, I'd rather not."

"Well, we'll contact his family. Do you know how we can reach them?"

Jack's hands were trembling as he checked his card files, found a card, scribbled a name and address on it and handed it to Lieutenant Williams.

Peter could see how completely stunned Jack was by this unexpected news. There was a carafe on the desk, so Peter filled a glass with cold water and handed it to Jack, who accepted it with a weak "Thanks."

Giving him time to adjust to the devastating news, both policemen took seats near Jack's desk.

"We're sorry to have to bring such news to you, but we're investigating this death as a homicide."

"A homicide? Why? Why would anyone want to kill Leroy?"

"We're hoping, sir, that you can help us. Please, just tell us what you know about your friend."

It turned out to be a familiar story. A very common, ordinary one. Two young men, one from Las Vegas and the other from Houston meet as roommates at Boston University. Their friendship extended beyond graduation, and as newcomers to the city of Boston, they recognized the need for a publication like *BAD*.

"We talked to our parents and relatives," Jack said, "and they agreed with us. We borrowed seed, or start up, money from them. My dad took out a second mortgage on our house in Houston and Leroy's dad maxed out his credit cards for us. Oh, God!" he stopped suddenly, his face contorted by what Peter thought was genuine grief. "Do I have to tell him about . . . about Leroy? How'm I going to do that?" The horror in his eyes seemed real.

John Williams spoke softly.

"We can do that," he said. "Notify his dad."

"My God, this news is going to kill his father. His mother is dead, and there's just the two of them. This is going to kill him!"

Lieutenant Williams touched him on his shoulder. "Sorry to bring such sad news. We may need to talk with you again."

"Anything. Anything," he murmured into his hands clutching his face. "Anything I can do to help." He dropped his hands from his pain-filled eyes to make another request.

"Please . . . please let me know when you've talked to Leroy's father. I want to let him know . . ." his voice trailed off.

"Will do," the lieutenant reassured him. "We'll let ourselves out."

As the two men walked down the long, winding staircase from Jack's office, each man was silent with thoughts about what they had just learned.

When they reached the parked cruiser, they got in and sat for a moment.

Lieutenant Williams broke the silence.

"Well?" He put the key into the ignition, but did not turn it on, waiting for Peter's answer.

"There's more to this than meets the eye and *I* think Jack Davona is in the middle of it somehow."

The lieutenant turned the key to start the car, looked at the rear view mirror before moving out into the street.

"I think you're right. Believe we ought to report to the chief of detectives. Case may become wider in scope than we thought. Already we're reaching outside of Boston."

"Getting to be a small, small world, Lieutenant."

As soon as the detectives left his office, Jack Davona slammed his fist down so hard on his desk that papers, pencils, even his half-filled glass of water shook and threatened to topple.

"Damn. Damn, why'd Leroy have to get himself killed?" Jack saw the far-reaching scheming, conniving hand of Gus Hodges in Leroy's murder. Why did he have Leroy offed? He'd been sending Hodges the payments each week, including the seven percent interest. Or had he? With that thought, he called his secretary on the intercom. "Bring me the files from Leroy Hayes's office, then lock the office door and bring me the key."

A few minutes later he heard the secretary wheeling the small wooden file cabinet down the corridor. He opened his office door to help her push it toward his desk. She also gave him the key to the late editor's office.

Angela Moss had been Jack's secretary since the start and knew that something very serious must have happened. She had realized that something was amiss since the police had come and gone. She was not surprised at Jack's next request.

"At ten-thirty," he consulted his watch, "I want every staff member here in my office, Mrs. Moss. Everyone!"

It was a sober-faced group of employees that trooped into Jack's large office/workroom. Were they going to be fired? Was *BAD* folding? Downsizing?

None of them was aware of the chief editor's sudden death. They formed confused clusters: editors, reporters, proofreaders, layout artists, and secretaries all waited to learn why they had been summoned.

Jack had stationed himself in front of his desk. The dark look on his face foretold of some horrible event that was verified as soon as he began to speak.

"The police just left this office and I have some very tragic news."

Audible gasps hissed through the staff as Jack's words took shape in their minds.

"Leroy Hayes, our chief editor and . . . and," his voice cracked with emotion, "one of my dearest, closest friends was found dead this morning."

Questions of disbelief and horror came all at once.

"Oh no!"

"What happened?"

"Where was he?"

Jack raised both hands to stop the flow of questions coming from his staff.

"All the police know at this point is that he was found early this morning in the park near the golf course with a bullet in the back of his head. Of course they are investigating it as a homicide. Marcia," he singled out Marcia Staples who was Leroy's assistant, "please take over in Leroy's place for the time being, will you?"

The tearful young editor nodded her head while wiping tears away. Another young editor had her arms around Marcia trying to comfort the grief-stricken assistant editor.

"And the rest of you, please carry on. As soon as I get further information, I'll pass it on. Thanks for continuing to do good work. I appreciate it."

Several of the older staffers who had been with Jack and Leroy since the inception of the magazine came forward to shake Jack's hand and murmur phrases of sympathy. He thanked each of them but his mind was swirling with questions.

Why was Leroy killed? Could it be the far-reaching hand of Gus Hodges that was responsible? Leroy had made all the arrangements with Hodges and assured Jack that everything was fine. But this morning's tragic news meant that everything was not fine. Damn it, if he'd been able to marry Sherissa, none of this would have happened. He would have had access to the money he needed.

Thirteen

The medical examiner's report of the postmortem examination of Leroy Hayes's body was on the lieutenant's desk when the two men returned from their meeting with Jack Davona.

John Williams read out loud to his sergeant some of the pertinent facts.

"Well, seemed our victim received a penetrating shot to the back of the head at close range. That means it was a deliberate execution and the gun was about two feet away from him."

"The doc get the bullet?"

"Yep. A .38. Left a large hole in the occipital area, back of the brain, and there was tattooing, gunpowder particles present, which means a close intentional killing."

"Think the victim knew his killer?" Peter wanted to know.

"I rather think so. There was no sign of a struggle, no scars, bruises, nothing under the nails. Nothing. Oh, oh," the lieutenant chuckled, "Peter, you've *got* to see this!"

Among the photographs of the victim's body was an enlargement of the front of his right thigh. In a column on the dead man's leg was tattooed a list of women's names, six in all, with a tattooed line crossing out each woman's name except for the last one, Jasmine.

Peter looked at the black and white photograph, read the names listed. He almost choked when he saw the name second from the bottom. Sheri. *Sheri,* what was her name doing on a dead man's thigh?

It was after twelve noon before an anxious Sergeant Peter Linwood could leave the police station to look into the shocking revelation of seeing Sheri's name on the dead man. He *had* to talk with her despite the lieutenant's warning about unethical social involvement.

As soon as he got into his car, seeking privacy from others that might overhear, he punched in her number on his cellular phone. There was no answer, except Sheri's voice that instructed him to—'Leave a message after the tone and I'll return your call. And do have a nice day.'

Yeah, right, he thought, *so far it's been real nice.*

He drove to The Good Egg where he ordered a BLT and Coke to go, and returned to his car. He was still shaken by what he had learned and decided to drive to the murder scene. He didn't know why he wanted to go but there was some nagging compulsion to do so.

When he arrived at the site it looked nothing like it had the previous day. No police around, no yellow tape cordoning off the area, and, of course, no dead body.

He sat in his car, eating his lunch, and noticed several golfers, a foursome, making their way across the green to the next tee, unaware, he was certain, of the tragedy that had taken place there. They were at ease, socializing, joking with one another, enjoying the glorious summer day while he tried to make sense of the stunning news that disturbed him. He *had* to hear from Sherissa.

When he returned to his desk, the lieutenant had news for him. Jared Hayes, the dead man's father, had been notified and was due to arrive at Logan Airport that afternoon. "We'll have him in for questioning as soon as he gets here to identify the body."

"Is there anything you want me to check on, Lieutenant?"

"Not at the moment, Pete. I'm expecting more info from forensics about the bullet and its markings."

He leaned back in his chair, looked across their two desks facing each other and told Peter, "One other thing. The medical examiner found a fifty-cent piece with a hole in it in the victim's pants pocket. Now we know this is a mob murder. And another thing, Pete," his kindly face softened, "don't think I missed your reaction this morning when you saw that name. I know you are upset over that. You have my permission to follow up . . . but keep it on a professional level."

"I'll do just that, John, just that," he said, relieved that he had permission to contact Sherissa. Of course he'd intended to anyway, but the lieutenant's permission eased his mind.

His telephone answering machine's light was blinking furiously as Peter entered his bedroom. He quickly shrugged off his blazer as he listened.

"Peter Linwood, this is Sherissa Holland. Please call me as soon as you get this message."

He dialed her number, relieved when she answered.

"Sherissa, I've been trying to reach you."

"Oh, yes, Peter, thanks for returning my call. I don't want to be a bother to you, but you did say . . ."

"Yes, it's no bother for you to call. What can I do for you?"

"Well, I remembered you said I could call and. . . ." He heard hesitation in her voice. "I didn't think he would do it but Jack has been calling me constantly. Wants us to get back together, and I've told him again and again that our relationship is over, the engagement called off, and he just keeps calling. Even if I don't answer he leaves messages. I've been thinking about some type of court order to keep him from bothering me."

"You could probably do that, although I don't put much faith in restraining orders."

"I thought as much. But I've got to do something. Now to make things worse, he's appealing to my sympathy. Left a message that Leroy Hayes was dead. Murdered, I think he said."

"Right. That's one of the things I wanted to talk about. Sheri, how well did you know Leroy Hayes?"

"I knew that he and Jack had been friends for years, were in the publishing of *BAD* together. We saw each other occasionally. Why do you ask?"

"Did you ever date him?" Peter blurted out, almost unable to wait for her answer.

"Date *him*? No, I never did. Why are you asking me that?"

Peter noticed that her tone of voice had risen sharply as if she was angry. "Are you sitting down?"

"Yes, I am," she declared.

"I don't know how to tell you this, but your name— well, Sheri—was found in a column of women's names tattooed on Leroy Hayes' right thigh. Every one of the six names, including Sheri, had a line tattooed through it except for the last one: Jasmine."

"Good God, man!" Sherissa exploded over the telephone. "I'm not the only girl in Boston, or anywhere else, with the nickname Sheri! Give me a break. First you tell me that I may have been an intended victim, someone out there might want to kill me, and now it could be *my* name tattooed on a dead man's thigh! Boy, are you out of your mind? Thought the police were supposed to help people!" She slammed down the receiver with a bang.

Peter groaned, still holding onto the receiver. He'd messed up again. She was right. He hadn't helped her at all . . . and he wanted to. Very badly. So very badly.

One of the police officers escorted Jared Hayes, a thin, gaunt man who walked into Lieutenant Williams's office with the unmistakable rolling gait of an old-time cowboy.

The lieutenant stood up to shake the man's hand.

"Lieutenant Williams, sir, and I'm very sorry about your loss."

"Thank you." Williams noted a definite western drawl in the man's words.

"Please, sir," he gestured, "have a seat."

With a deep sigh, the gray-haired, nut-brown-skinned man placed his overnight bag on the floor beside the chair and sat down slowly, placing his hat and raincoat on his bag. He looked around the squad room, seemingly wondering why he was in such an unfamiliar place, as if he were a displaced person in a foreign land. Obviously he was still in shock over the sorrowful task he had just completed, identifying his dead son.

This part of police work was a part that Williams never relished, dealing with bereaved relatives. But over the years he had found it best to remain calm and matter of fact. It was a time to be as normal as possible, considering the circumstances. So he asked his visitor, "May I get you something to drink? Coffee? A cold drink?"

"Black coffee would be okay. Please."

"Coming right up."

The murdered victim's father gratefully sipped the hot coffee for a few minutes, and Williams allowed him the time to collect himself. Finally the man asked him, "Do you know what happened to my son? Who killed him?" He took a few more swallows of coffee, held the cup in his hand as if to warm his fingers, and waited for an answer.

"At the present moment, I do not. From what little evidence we have, we believe it may have been a mob hit, has several indications of such."

Hearing those words, the distraught father put his coffee cup on the desk and stared at him.

"A mob hit, you say?"

"So far, Mr. Hayes, what evidence we have points in that direction. We're still searching for more information. I know this is a bad time for you, and you've had recent health problems yourself, but any information you can give us about your son would be helpful."

"Tell you whatever you want to know."

The lieutenant reached for a legal pad of paper.

"Your son was not married?"

"Not that I know of. Always had plenty of girl-friends."

The detective nodded as he made notes on the yellow sheet of paper, remembering the tattooed list of names.

"And he worked closely with Jack Davona?"

"Oh, yes, he and Jack were good friends, back to their college days."

"Have you been in touch with Jack?"

"He called me in Las Vegas to express his sympathy.

I asked him to book a room for me at a hotel and I'm going to go there when I leave here."

"Be glad to have a plainclothes officer take you. Which hotel?"

"Believe it's the Stargate Plaza." He consulted a card that he took from his wallet. "Yes. Stargate Plaza on Tremont Street."

"No problem. I'll see that you get there. Is this your first visit to Boston?"

"Yes."

"Sorry it's on such a sad occasion."

"Jack said something about a memorial service and I asked him to find a funeral director. My son will be cremated, and then," his voice cracked and his dark eyes filled with tears as he spoke the next few words, "I'll be taking my son back to Las Vegas in an urn to bury him beside his mother."

Fourteen

"So, she slammed the phone down on you?"

"She was hotter than a firecracker, and I haven't been able to reach her since. I'm worried, too," Peter admitted to his superior officer, "because she said Jack Davona was bothering her with nonstop phone calls, pressing her to renew their engagement. Told me she was considering a restraining order."

"He's harassing her that much, eh?"

"That's what she told me. So, I called the television station and they said she was on emergency leave. Even though I reminded them that I was a police officer investigating a homicide, they wouldn't say what kind of emergency or when she would return to work."

"Hmmm. I do remember, Peter, that when she got the job at WHAB the *Boston Globe* did quite a write up on her. First woman of color hired, etcetera. You know. And I seem to remember reading that she had a twin brother, a basketball coach at some college in Maryland. Maybe that's where she went. Understand they're very close."

"Thanks, I'll check into that. How did you make out with Mr. Hayes?"

"From what he told me, I believe Jack Davona is somehow in the middle of this set of circumstances."

"That so?" Peter had similar thoughts about Jack Davona and was eager to learn what the lieutenant had discovered.

"To begin with, 'Sonny,' as Mr. Hayes calls his son, is not his biological son."

"He's adopted?"

"The father told me that he and his wife were never able to have children so they adopted Leroy when he was almost four. When they adopted him they found out that he had been in various foster homes until he became eligible for a legal adoption. And the only thing they were ever able to learn about their son's biological parents was that they were unmarried teenagers. He said they never made any attempt to contact the young people. Leroy didn't want to know, Mr. Hayes said, and they respected his wishes. Said he considered his wife, Tammy, and him as his folks.

"So Leroy Hayes never knew his real parents?"

"According to Mr. Hayes, the kid never wanted to find out, and Mr. Hayes told me that his wife was happy with that decision. Never had any difficulties with him. Not until later when his son got involved with a dude from the Caribbean."

"Began to wonder then what kind of genes the kid had, I guess," Peter offered.

"Something like that. Said up to that time, the teen years, you know, never had a bit of trouble, even growing up in a crazy city like Vegas where gambling and a fast lifestyle are par for the course. Boy did well in school, was good in sports, played baseball, ran track, and during summer vacations sometimes worked with him at the Sands or other hotels. Met big stars like Sammy Davis, Jr., Frank Sinatra, Steve Allen. Of course he was just a kid, but he took it all in stride the father told me."

Peter said, "I've been to Las Vegas several times and with all the gamblers, con men, crooks, and chorus girls don't see how anyone working around in that atmosphere could have a normal life. Too much for me!"

"I expect some families do stay intact and normal, but it must be hard to do."

"But then, Peter, Mr. Hayes told me something about his son that got my attention."

At that critical moment, Peter's telephone rang. He answered.

"Peter Linwood . . . yes, I do want that information . . . as soon as possible. Bye."

He leaned forward, anxious to hear the rest of John's information.

"Sorry about that, checking on Miss Holland's brother's address. So, what got your attention?"

"He said his son got involved somehow with a slick-talking dude named Gus Hodges. The kid was a senior in high school, had already been accepted at Boston University when the 'you know what' hit the fan! The kid was working as a mule for this Gus character, delivering drugs."

"Is there a yellow sheet on him?"

"Apparently not. Guess because he had no priors, good family, well known in the community, good student record, good work history. His father got a lawyer and by the end of the situation, the kid got off with a suspended sentence. Had to perform some community service, and because he was seventeen, his record was sealed. But, Pete, here's the kicker."

"What?"

"Mr. Hayes didn't find out until after his son was away at college that his high-priced lawyer had waived his fee. He said his intention was to pay the bill by remortgaging his house, kept waiting for a bill. Finally he went to the lawyer, was told that the lawyer had tried the case pro bono, wanting to help a young brother out of a jam. The lawyer was on Gus Hodges' payroll."

"So," Peter interjected, "he wasn't aware of the gangster's involvement or of ABH Enterprises?"

"Said he wasn't. Had never heard of them. He and his wife were ecstatic when the situation was cleared up and their son went off to college. He said the boy was his mother's heart and she died shortly after, believing that all was well. She had been happy about his friendship with Jack Davona, whom she loved like a son, too. He said that was one reason he was more than willing to help the two of them with the start up costs of *BAD,* their new venture. He maxed out his credit cards to get money for them."

"So when did he find out about ABH Enterprises?"

"When he gave them added funds for the magazine, he was told to make the check out to that name, thought it was their business name or something like that," John explained to his co-worker.

"That's really some story. Didn't know his son was still into the gangster."

"That's right, Peter. And I expect we are going to find out more as soon as I get some word from the Chicago police. I have a gut feeling that somehow the long arm of Gus Hodges has somehow reached Boston." He stood up. "I'm ready for lunch, how 'bout you?"

At The Good Egg they ran into the Chief of Detectives, Fran Muldonney, a sixty-year-old seasoned police officer who was looking forward to retirement in a few years.

"How's your investigation coming?" he asked John

Williams after popping a large potato chip into his mouth. He waved a pickle spear at them. "Understand you've contacted Chicago."

"That's right, Chief," John answered. "Got some promising leads we're checking out with them."

"Good, good. Keep at it."

"Will do, sir." John gave the chief a mock salute and both he and Peter went to the deli counter to order their lunch.

Luckily they found an empty table for two in a quiet corner where they sat down to wait for their orders to be brought over to them by the waitress. Nancy was already moving toward them with their beverages, iced tea with lemon for the lieutenant, and sparkling water for Peter.

"Gentlemen, your drinks."

"Thanks, Nancy," Peter said.

"You're welcome, Sarge."

Within a few minutes she brought their sandwiches back. The lieutenant had settled for a tuna salad, and Peter, knowing he probably would eat lightly when he got home that evening, had ordered a meatball submarine sandwich.

They ate silently, each man thinking about Mr. Jared Hayes and his dead son.

Fifteen

When Peter made the call, he was not surprised to hear a man's voice on the other end. He suspected that perhaps Sherissa, if she was at her brother's house, would be keeping a low profile.

"This is Todd Holland."

"Mr. Holland, my name is Sergeant Peter Linwood of the Boston Police Homicide Division."

"Yes, Sergeant, what can I do for you?"

There was a crispness to the man's voice which alerted Peter that he'd better state his message briefly and clearly.

"I am sorry to bother you, Mr. Holland, but I am investigating a hit and run accident which your sister, Miss Sherissa Holland, witnessed. I know she is distressed over this incident and I am concerned about her welfare. I recognize, too, that she has been upset about the behavior of her former fiancé, Jack Davona."

"Thank you for your concern."

"Your sister is safe then, I take it."

"Quite safe, Sergeant."

The man's response indicated to Peter that he was not inclined to offer more information, but Peter pressed on with his ultimate purpose.

"I would appreciate it, sir, if you would tell Miss

Holland that I called. Would you let her know that I apologize if I upset her with my telephone call the other day. Please let her know I am sorry. And my apologies for disturbing you."

"No problem, Sergeant."

"Goodbye, sir."

"Goodbye."

A click of the receiver in Peter's ear ended the conversation. Was Sherissa safe, really? Could he trust her brother? He realized he had to, he had no other choice. As he went over the conversation in his mind, he realized that Todd had offered little or no information. And if he allowed it, his worry over her safety might interfere with his work. The lieutenant was right. He should not become personally involved in his investigative work, but . . . it was too late for that warning.

One thing for sure, the case was becoming complicated. Had John Williams heard from Chicago? What did this Hodges dude have to do with anything? A mob hit, the lieutenant had indicated, was suspected in Leroy Hayes' murder. Did his death have anything to do with the boxer's hit and run death? Peter didn't know why, but he had a gut feeling that the two incidents were related. But how?

When he arrived at the police station the next morning, he was greeted by the usual cacophony of phones ringing, keyboards clacking, the blue monitors of computers with their ever-streaming data, plus the harried, strident voices of the police officers tending to their official duties. This was the milieu that Peter loved. Despite his abhorrence of dead bodies, it was the hunt, the chase, the problem-solving that appealed to him. It was also the opportunity to right a wrong, to bring some measure of justice to a grief-stricken family.

John Williams was already at his desk.

"Mornin'," he said to Peter.

"Mornin', John. What's new?"

"Well, this fax came in last night from Chicago. I'll let you look it over, but some major facts have come to light. ABH Enterprises *is* owned by one Augustus Bell Hodges, who has been a previous guest of one of Uncle Sam's finest federal prisons.

"For?" Peter wanted to know.

"Drug trafficking, money laundering, illegal gambling, for starters. Suspected of hiding funds in banks abroad and the islands. And, at one time, lived in Vegas. I figure he may have made friends with more than one high-priced lawyer who would be on his payroll."

Peter tapped his pen on a legal yellow pad where he had scribbled some notes as John talked.

"Hmmm. Las Vegas was Leroy Hayes's hometown." Idly he drew a small triangle on the pad and wrote initials of Hodges, Hayes, and Davona at each corner, ABH at the top, with LH and JD at the other two angles. He passed the diagram over to his partner, who nodded his head in agreement.

"You may be on to something. This could be the start we're looking for."

Peter pressed on. "John, we know Jack Davona needed money, was desperate for funds, had sworn that he would not let *BAD* go under. Maybe that's why he wanted to marry Sherissa, get access to some of her family's money. Probably thought the old man would come through for his daughter. Then when she reneged, changed her mind and broke off with him, he *had* to find another source."

"And maybe that's where Leroy Hayes comes in," John interrupted. "From what his father told me" he continued, "Hodges never let Leroy forget the debt he owned Hodges for getting the lawyer that took care of Leroy's teenage problem."

"So," Peter interjected excitedly, "if Hodges could launder his drug money through *BAD* publications . . ."

"Could be that was his goal. Jack needed money, Leroy owed Hodges, and Hodges needed to make his money legit. Maybe, just maybe, the three of them are in bed together."

"We need to get a hold of some records . . . start checking this out," Peter said.

"There's another thing, too, Peter," John said. "We know a Mercedes was somehow involved in both incidents. I want you to check owners of Mercedes here in Roxbury and Dorchester."

"Get on it right away."

"Good," John said. "I'm going to put in a call to Chicago. Have a few more questions that I need to ask. May even fly out there."

Sherissa came into Todd's living room. Her face was flushed and she seemed to be slightly out of breath.

"Jogging here in Maryland's not like jogging back home," she said to her brother as she flopped down on the couch. "Whew! It's so hot!"

"Ain't seen nothin' yet," Todd told her. "Wait until the humidity hits. Then you'll see what hot weather's really like! By the way," he said casually, "you had a phone call." He watched her very carefully, curious to watch her reaction when he told her about Peter's call.

"Who called? My producer?" Her eyebrows rose as question marks as she waited for his answer.

"No, not your boss. A Boston detective named Peter Linwood."

"Peter! What'd *he* want?" She sat straight up.

"Said he wanted to be sure you were safe and to tell you he was sorry if he upset you. Did he? Upset you, that is."

She shook her head. "Not really. I expect he was—is—concerned about me."

"Seems like a nice enough guy."

"Maybe," Sherissa admitted. It wasn't necessary for her brother to know how she really felt. *Then again,* she thought, *I don't really know how I really feel.*

Tyree was nervous. He had reason to be. Last night Mr. A.B. decided that he had to have "some real food that taste like back home." Tyree was driving to the south side of the city to pick up his boss's order of curry goat and rice, fried plantain, jerked chicken, some toss-em up salad, and meat patties. Tyree knew that such a diet had been forbidden by the doctors who tried to oversee Mr. A.B.'s health, but ever so often the man wanted a taste of home, and who was Tyree to deny him? He did as he was told. But when he saw an unfamiliar car moving slowly down the street as he drove out of the driveway, his antenna went up, and the hair prickled on the back of his neck. To his practiced eye the two men in the front of the car looked like cops. It was a gray Mazda, and Tyree knew he'd recognize it if he saw it again.

He drove very carefully, changing his route to be sure he wasn't followed, although he figured it wouldn't do much good. They already knew where he lived. But it didn't hurt to keep up his skills in evading the police.

He explained to his boss when he returned.

"Spotted the fuzz when I left, so I figured I'd shake 'em off. Took a long way round to Pop Collins's," referring to the West Indian restaurant where he'd picked up the food. "Figure they was casin' the place."

"Screw the friggin' fuzz!" Augustus snarled. "Got nothin' on me! Let's eat!"

But Tyree was correct. John Williams and one of his counterparts from the Chicago homicide division had driven by Hodges's ornate brick residence and had noticed Tyree as he drove out of the driveway.

Vincent Parsons, the Chicago detective, identified Tyree for John Williams.

"Tyree Embrey, Hodges's right-hand man. Live together, don't know if it's a sex thing, or if he's Hodges's protégé, pseudo-son, heir, or what. Been livin' here together 'bout five years."

"Got a rap sheet?"

"Yeah. NCIC's got a record on him," Detective Parsons said, referring to the National Crime Information Center.

"I'd like to see it," John said.

"No problem. I'll see that you have a copy."

"Thanks. You know, Vincent, just maybe this Tyree could be vulnerable. I mean, you say he has a rap sheet, small stuff, I expect, not having seen his record, and maybe he's flattered by his association with Gus Hodges."

Vincent Parsons negotiated around the traffic, complaining, "The mayor's got to do something about this traffic gridlock. Good thing we're not in a hurry. Hate to use the siren."

"'Know what you mean," John concurred. "Sometimes it makes it worse."

"Right. But back to this Tyree guy. Could very well

be that he *is* in over his head. Could be the Achilles' heel. What say we rattle his cage, see what falls out?"

"In the meantime, think you could put a spotlight on him?" John suggested.

"Will do. Now, let's go see what we can pull up on the young man's record," Vincent said as he drove into the police headquarters parking lot.

Sixteen

Peter found the car that had been involved in both the crimes that he and John Williams were investigating and he was in a hurry to let John know. He phoned the Chicago hotel.

John Williams grinned when he heard the breathless excitement in his sergeant's voice.

"Yo, John! We found it!"

"The Mercedes?"

"Yep."

"How do you know it's the right one?"

"Forensics. They came up with the proof. Fibers from the boxer's sweats that were embedded in the grill match, the Michelin tire tracks match the cast of the tire tracks at the scene, and the soil samples are the same from the tires and the road."

"Good."

"Yeah, right, but you'll never guess where we located the vehicle."

"No, I don't think so. So tell me, where?"

"In Jack Davona's garage!"

"Davona?"

"Damn straight. I had checked all the owners of Mercedes sold in the Boston area in the past two years and when I saw Jack Davona's name on the list, I knew

I'd struck pay dirt! Got a warrant to search his garage."

"And the car was there?" John asked.

"Right."

"What was his reaction?"

"Oh, man! You should have seen him. Sweatin' big time! 'Don't know anything 'bout any accident or who murdered Leroy,' he said. He was plenty nervous, let me tell you."

"I bet he was. What else did he say?"

"John, he blustered and tried to put on a good face. You know, a big-time magazine publisher: 'Wasn't even in town, don't you know, when that boxer was killed . . . haven't used my Mercedes since I've been back.' He went on and on acting as if I was some kind of nut for even suggesting such a thing. And then I told him somebody drove his car in his absence. *That's* when he stopped rantin' and ravin', a funny look came over his face."

"Like he was scared?"

"No, John, more like someone had hit him on the head with a two-by-four and, like, it suddenly dawned on him that maybe he was in trouble big time. He had to sit down he was so nervous."

"Did you ask him who drove the car?"

"Oh, you bet I did! He kept sayin' 'Wasn't here, I tell you! I can prove that I was in California. I did not drive that car that night.' And then I told him that we had already gone over the car thoroughly, finger-printed it, and it was only a matter of time before we would know who drove the car. That's when he admitted that he had given the keys to someone else."

"Who? Who?"

"The second victim, Leroy Hayes."

"Leroy Hayes? Did you confirm that?"

"Oh, yeah. Cotton fibers found in the driver's seat match fibers from the Harvard sweat suit Leroy Hayes was wearing. Must have worn it that night."

John Williams was thinking about what Peter was telling him.

"So," he said to Peter, "somebody wanted Leroy Hayes dead. Got him to off the boxer—then killed *him*. I wonder who and why. Anyway, real good work, Pete. You've given me something to work on and the answers just may be here in the Windy City."

"Anything happenin' out there?" Peter wanted to know.

"I'm checkin' some leads, but getting back to Jack Davona, I think you better subpoena his financial records and bank statements. We'll want to follow the money trail and I have the feeling it's between Las Vegas and Chicago."

"Could very well be, John. Anything else you want me to look into?"

"Can't think of anything at the moment. If I do, I'll call you. I expect to be back in a few days."

He hung up the telephone and reached for the room service menu card. He would order a meal to be brought to his room, he had a lot of thinking to do. The triangular relationship between the three major players seemed stronger than ever. And one of them was dead. Would there be more deaths?

Gus Hodges was a villain and he did not care who knew what he was. He never worried about how other people viewed him. Back in the small Caribbean island of his birth, he'd left a wife and four children. "Man," he'd say, "they drag down on me, so I get meself shut of them. Got no time to be so burdened!"

His goal was to make money and he was proud that he, Gus Hodges, a black lad from a banana plantation had enough smarts to make it. His well-established drug cartel extended from the tiny windward island to the gambling houses of Las Vegas to the grimy streets of south-side Chicago and even to the offices of stately, eloquent Swiss bankers. They all had served him well. He was a ruthless man, especially in his dealings with others. He wanted everything to go his way and any who crossed him paid dearly—most often with their lives. No one received a second chance. His underlings in each of these locations moved to do his bidding whenever he called, knowing they were going to be well compensated when they succeeded in their assigned tasks.

The nervous tension that Tyree had been suffering since he had noticed the detectives in their unmarked car was beginning to disturb him. He mentioned to Mr. A.B. that he believed the house was being monitored.

"They wearin' plain clothes, but I know a tin man when I see one," Tyree stated.

Gus Hodges was not unaware of his protege's anxiety level. Indeed, for the past six months or so, he wondered if he should continue their present relationship. Perhaps the time had come to make changes. Gus could not stomach weak, indecisive, wishy-washy behavior. Tyree had not acted like this before, but perhaps the recent events in Boston had unnerved him.

They were in Hodges's ornate living room which he had furnished with heavy Victorian furniture of oak and mahogany. Paintings by Picasso, Monet, and

other artists were displayed on dark walls with special
lighting focused on each one. The oriental rugs on
the floor had been handwoven in Kazakhstan. Their
bright warm colors somewhat relieved the heavy
somber feeling the room presented. Tyree was never
at ease in this room, but Gus reveled in it. It was what
gave the mobster a feeling of entitlement and pres-
tige, as if he was, as they say, to the manor born.

The man settled back in his favorite dark green vel-
vet upholstered wing chair, placed his feet on a
matching ottoman, and motioned to Tyree to fetch
his favorite rum drink. Under his heavy-lidded eyes in
his large bland face he observed how tense and worried Tyree had become. No doubt about it. The kid
was scared and becoming unraveled. Time for him
to go, and the sooner the better. No longer valuable
to him, the kid could be a big liability. Quickly, Gus
made up his mind.

"Wanna get outta town for a few days?" he asked
Tyree as he accepted his drink. He did not miss the
relieved surprise on his aide's face.

"Want me to go someplace, boss?"

"Yes. I'm expecting a package delivery in Las Vegas.
Want you to pick it up. In my office there's a large
manila envelope on my desk. Bring it to me."

Once Tyree had returned with the envelope, Gus
put his drink on the table beside his chair and proceeded to give instructions.

"Pack only an overnight bag. I want you to pick up
the package an' come back straight away."

"Yes, sir."

He pulled an airplane ticket folder out of the envelope, handed it to Tyree.

"This is your flight ticket." Gus was pleased with

himself that he had planned ahead for this turn of events. He went on to explain to Tyree.

"Everything is in this packet. All the instructions and everything you need to know. Now you better go and pack. There'll be a cab at the back of the house in a half hour to take you to the airport."

Things had moved swiftly for Tyree, but he was accustomed to Gus's method of doing things so he wasn't rattled by this turn of events. Secretly, he was glad to be leaving Chicago, but he did ask his employer, "You goin' be okay here by yourself, boss?"

Gus threw back his head with an uproarious laugh. "Who said I was goin' be *alone?*" he quipped.

"Right, sir," Tyree said, understanding that Mr. A.B. never lacked for companionship, particularly of the female persuasion.

As soon as Tyree left the room, Gus picked up the telephone and dialed a number.

"Ten-fifteen flight to Vegas," he said to the listener on the other end. He sighed when he placed the phone back in its cradle. He'd had great hopes for the boy, but after five years the kid had gotten weak. So be it. He'd have to start grooming someone else.

Seventeen

Wearing dark gray slacks with a navy blazer, Tyree settled into his seat on the plane and breathed a sigh of relief. He'd be a dead man for sure if Gus ever discovered he'd been questioned by the police. But what could he do? When the police stopped him, saying his taillight was out, he knew they were lying. But he had to answer their questions, especially after they threatened to take him downtown. As he sat in the plane awaiting takeoff, he realized that he had made a great mistake by not phoning one of Gus's lawyers for advice, but he thought he could handle the situation by himself. Even when the police told him, "We've had access to your boss's phone records and we know that a call was made to Boston and we know that as a result of that call two men are dead," he tried to bluff his way out.

"I don't know anything about anything! I made a call for my boss and delivered a message. That's all I did!" he had insisted. He recalled every moment of the encounter.

Vincent Parsons's face flushed to a deep, angry red. He turned to John Williams.

"The law says *this* man can be charged as an accessory to murder, isn't that true, Lieutenant?" Then he explained to Tyree that Lieutenant John Williams of the Boston Police Department was here in Chicago investigating a murder case and trying to determine if there was a Chicago connection.

Tyree had watched as the Boston policeman nodded his head in agreement.

"He's right, son. May have to extradite you back to Massachusetts to stand trial for murder."

"Why'd you stop me, anyway? My taillights ain't out!" Tyree's eyes bugged out of his head like a bullfrog on a lily pad. Perspiration beaded on his forehead and began dripping down the sides of his nose.

John Williams felt sorry for him, but not for long. He was certain this young man was somehow involved in the events that had occurred in Boston. He listened as Vincent Parsons, a large, well-built man with a marine-type haircut for his stiff red hair, began his interrogation. His deep voice boomed authoritatively, evidence of his strong Nordic heritage. He was an officer not to be trifled with, and John wondered if Tyree had recognized that yet.

Parsons asked for his license and registration. Tyree continued to protest while searching the glove compartment for the necessary documents.

"I've never killed anyone, I tell you! All's I did was make a call to Leroy Hayes and deliver my boss's message. You got nothin' on me!" he blustered. "Get outta my face!" he demanded.

Reliving the experience all over again as he sat waiting for takeoff, he realized that his relationship with Augustus Bell Hodges had come to an abrupt end. Damn, what would he do now? Could he offer his good looks and obsequious manners to someone else who would support him in the style he wanted *and* needed?

A tall, dark-brown man who resembled a very famous

basketball player came down the aisle breathlessly to take the empty seat beside Tyree.

"Oh, man," he huffed, "almost didn't make the flight. Getting too old to manage these close calls."

"Know what you mean," Tyree said. He picked up the in-flight magazine and began to read. He was too nervous to really concentrate so as soon as the plane was airborne, he pushed his seat back a little and tried to sleep. Many others on the plane did the same as the plane roared through the dark night on its way to the city of hopes and dreams. And just like many other cities, it was also a place of violence and murder.

The medical examiner's written report of the autopsy on the body found on the airplane began with this statement: *Postmortem exam reveals a UBM, WD, WN, approximately 30 y/o.* Officials who read the report understood that it was about an unknown black male, well-dressed and well-nourished, who was about thirty years old.

The report continued to state that no obvious physical injuries were noted. Stomach contents were normal with no trace of alcohol. Further investigation, however, revealed an injection site on the victim's left anterior femur. Hemoanalysis indicated the presence of toxic poisons. Conclusion: Cause of Death—lethal injection by person or persons unknown.

The large man with the resemblance to a basketball player was one of the first passengers off the plane. He was carrying an overnight bag and had a manila envelope under his arm. His size was intimidating to other passengers who quickly made way for him.

* * *

Gus Hodges checked his E-mail first thing the next morning. A woman, a long-time friend who had shared his bed, was still sleeping, which was just as well because he was anxious to know if his latest order had been carried out.

As he scrolled down and read his messages, he said, "A-ha," as he read the one he'd expected: DELIVERY COMPLETE AS ORDERED.

It was signed by a code name he recognized. Sighing deeply, he rose from his desk, pulled the belt of his dressing gown tighter around his sagging abdomen and padded down the hall to the kitchen to make a pot of coffee. His maid would be in later. He'd told her not to come in until noon. He'd planned that the Tyree business would be concluded by then and his lady friend would have gone home. The pungent smell of coffee would wake her, he knew, and if it didn't he'd take a fresh steaming cup to her bedside. That would do it. As soon as he got her out of the house, he had urgent business to take care of, the sooner the better. Too bad about Tyree but, as he'd often told him, "Man, you can't let *anybody* drag on you, pull you down," and the lad had been surely heading in that direction.

"Vincent, want to thank you for your help. Think we've got a handle on our Boston problems."

"Glad to help a fellow officer," Vincent Parsons responded agreeably. "Still want us to keep an eye on Gus?"

"Yes, if you could. Somehow I believe he is the key to this whole thing."

"Right, John. We've been aware for some time that

there could be a possibility that he was involved in drugs or some other nefarious activity and he's aware, too, that we've been on the alert where he is concerned."

They were sitting in the office of the Chicago police detective which was much like Williams's office back in Boston. Same desks, same cacophony of police-related noises and the same inevitable constantly brewing coffee pot. "Would you like more coffee?"

"Thanks, no, I'm fine," John said. He took another sip of his coffee, leaned back in his chair, pulled at his chin with his left hand. "I wonder," he said slowly, "is there a possibility you could subpoena his bank records and tax records? You see, *I* think there's a relationship between him and Jack Davona, the publisher of the magazine *BAD*. I know Davona needed money, even went out of town, flying all over, to find some venture capitalists to back him. His 'friend', second in command, Leroy Hayes, was beholden to Gus Hodges, some skirmish the kid got into, and Gus with *his* lawyer got the kid out of it. But knowing how these crooks act, Gus may have called in his markers. My sergeant thinks Davona's ex-fiancé was the intended target."

"And this Leroy guy hit the boxer by mistake?"

"That's right. He was a welterweight, see, weighed about 145 pounds, and dressed in dark sweats. It was a very dark, rainy morning. The car had no lights on, could be he mistook the boxer for the girl. Anyway, that's what my sergeant thinks and I'm inclined to agree with him."

"But, then," Vincent added, "when Gus found out that this Leroy fellow had goofed, he had him taken out. Cruel son of a bitch, right?"

"In my book, one of the cruelest. That's why I have to put him away."

"Rest assured, John, we'll do whatever it takes on this end," Vincent said. "We have Tyree's admission that he made the phone call for Hodges. As far as I'm concerned, that started the whole sequence of events."

"I agree," John concurred, rising from his seat, straightening his trouser leg with a quick shake of his foot as he did so.

"I'm certain that I can get a warrant from one of the judges to subpoena Hodges's financial records, particularly when I let the judge know we're looking into a money laundering scheme, as well as murder." Vincent Parsons jotted down a reminder for himself on a pad of paper, then looked up from his desk at John, who was preparing to leave.

"You know, my surveillance team tells me that there's been no sign of Tyree Embrey these past few days. They've spotted women going in and out of the Hodges place, but no Tyree."

"Maybe he's out of town," John said.

"Maybe. And maybe that's another question I'll have for Gus Hodges, you know?" He rose from his chair, reached over to shake hands with John.

"Have a safe trip back to Boston."

"Will do. Keep in touch, and thanks for all your help."

"No problem. *Our* motto is the same: Protect and serve, eh? That's what we're doing."

Eighteen

"I've got to go home, Todd. I only asked for a week's leave and Mr. Osgood said he *did* understand that I needed some time . . ."

"But what about Jack? Will he still bother you?"

"Oh, I don't think so. He's got to know our relationship is over."

Todd still felt great concern for his sister's welfare but he did not want to cast doubts on her sense of independence or self-sufficiency, but the inquiries he had made about Jack Davona, about his dealings with Leroy Hayes and quite possibly Gus Hodges, worried him. He did not want to tell his sister what he had learned but he intended to have someone keep an eye out for his twin.

As if aware of his doubt for her well-being, she told him, "You know, Todd, I've already changed all the locks on the doors, upgraded my alarm system, and I have an unlisted phone number. And Peter Linwood has given me his phone number and his beeper number so that I can get in touch with him if I need to."

"Uh-huh," Todd grunted, but he persisted. "Look, Sheri, I know you are a sensible girl and can pretty much take care of yourself, but don't mind me if I worry a little bit." He put his arm around her and hugged her close. "And if you should need *more* muscle, you can always call on Elijah. That tall African would make anyone who tried to bother you think twice.

Sherissa was glad when she got back to Boston to return to her job and pick up her life again. She took a shuttle flight from Baltimore to Boston and the very first thing she did was pick up Zeus from the animal shelter where she had boarded him while she was away. The attendant brought him out to her.

"This is one feisty cat, you have, ma'am," the attendant said when she handed Zeus over in his traveling carrier.

"Gave you trouble, did he? Zeus, you naughty cat! I know he's spoiled rotten," she told the young girl as she wrote out a check, "but he is my best friend, aren't you, Zeus? And I've had him since he was a kitten."

"He may be just a cat but he lives up to his name, god of all he surveys," the girl said. "Goodbye, Zeus, come see us again."

"Thanks, Miss," Sherissa said.

"Anytime, Miss Holland. Glad to have him, even if he is a little bossy."

As soon as she returned to her home, she opened the windows in the living room to air out the closed-in, stuffy room. She then poured some of Zeus' favorite treats into his bowl, which he devoured hungrily. Then he walked into her bedroom, jumped up on the foot of her bed where he stretched and yawned, then curled up into a ball and promptly fell asleep. Watching him made Sherissa smile. *I know*, she said silently. *There's no place like home.*

After she made a pot of fresh coffee, she poured a

cup and carried it into her living room. She always felt relaxed in this cozy, quiet place surrounded by things she loved: her Chinese lacquered chest, the small tables on either side of her damask-covered loveseat, with gold and red enamel surfaces reflected by the light that filtered through the muted silk beige shades. The Chinese rug that covered the floor was thick and pleasing when she kicked off her shoes and curled her toes over it. The sensation calmed her.

As she sat, sipping her coffee, she began to review the disturbing circumstances that had upset her previously placid life. It had all started when she thought she loved Jack. Now she wondered: How could she have believed she loved him? Now, almost too late, she realized that she could not love a man whose principles and ideals did not and could not agree with hers. And there was his relationship with Leroy. She had never trusted *him*. He came across to her as a pathological liar. It seemed to her that he had a crafty look in his eyes and she never felt that Jack's best friend was trustworthy. And to think there was a possibility that *her* name had been tattooed on his leg. She shivered with distaste and horror at the thought. Why would he do such a thing? Was he trying to get back at Jack for something? Why Jack trusted Leroy she never understood. Jack insisted his friend was a 'good old boy' from back home. Maybe something strange had occurred back home in Texas. She thought of what Peter Linwood had suggested . . . that perhaps *she* was the intended victim. But who would want her dead . . . and why?

Thinking of the detective, she wondered how the case was progressing. She wondered, too, if she should let him know that she'd received his apology and that she was back in Boston?

* * *

Peter Linwood had Sherissa Holland on *his* mind, but he knew she was off limits until the case had been solved and brought to trial.

When he arrived at the station, John Williams was at his desk. He was glad to see him.

"John, you're back." The two men shook hands, genuinely glad to see each other.

"Got in last night from Chicago, Pete. It was quite a trip and I think we're going to make headway on this case."

"You do?" Peter's excitement showed in his face.

"Yep," John grinned at his young partner, "I think we're on a fast track. Met an officer named Vincent Parsons and he's goin' to be workin' with us back in Chicago. Let me lay it on you, kid."

"You got my undivided attention, John. I can't wait."

"Go get yourself a cuppa and bring me one, too, and I'll talk."

Peter returned with two steaming cups of coffee, placed one in front of the lieutenant and sat down at his desk. He took a tentative sip of the liquid and decided it was too hot to drink.

"Better let this cool a bit," he told John who was emptying a creamer into his own cup of hot coffee.

"Well, this is what I found out. Gus Hodges has a young aide, protégé, go-fer, right-hand man, living with him in Chicago. Lived, that is. But I'll get to that later. Anyway, we stopped him one night, Parsons and I, taillight out, you know, and when we subsequently upset him, telling him he had to go down to the precinct, he stopped blustering about being stopped for DWB, as he called it, driving while black, but we assured him that it was none of that but that we knew that he had made calls to Boston. And when Vincent Parsons identified *me* as a Boston detective, Tyree became very talkative."

"He admitted he made the phone call?"

"Pete, he was glad to admit to that. Kept sayin' 'only made a phone call, didn't *kill* nobody!' I tell you, son, I can't believe that a con man as smart and as crafty as Hodges would have tied himself up with such a flake as Tyree."

"Maybe Hodges had other scummy reasons," Peter suggested.

"Right, could be. Anyway, Tyree was happy finally to admit that he had made calls to Boston at his boss's request."

"Then what did you find out?" Peter was anxious, could hardly wait to hear what other evidence his partner had discovered.

"Well," John leaned back against his chair and began to tap his pencil against the yellow legal pad on his desk. He knew how anxious Peter was to find out what he had learned in Chicago. He remembered he'd felt the same way when he was a young detective. He went on with his findings.

"You remember after my talk with Leroy's dad we found out that Leroy owed Gus, and so *I* think it is safe to assume that Leroy was ordered to kill the girl."

"Why do you think Gus wanted the girl dead?" The thought of Sherissa being harmed made the hairs raise at the back of his neck, and without even being aware of it, his stomach formed knots and his fists tightly clenched. He pictured her in his mind, her soft smooth skin that he'd wanted to touch so badly the few times he was near her. Her sweet lithe body that he ached to hold, to comfort her, protect her, to know as he did his own. Would Fate grant him such a treasure? He could almost taste the sweetness that he knew her lips would offer if only he could claim them with his own. After only a few brief contacts, he knew this desirable young woman was the one he wanted to share his life. He could not exist without her in his life and as soon as this case was settled, by God, he intended to pursue that goal. To think that someone wanted to harm her—he forced his mind back to what the lieutenant was saying.

". . . so I'm assuming, Peter, knowing how Hodges operates, that he needed a way to launder his drug money, and what better way than by owning a legitimate business? So here's what we know. Jack Davona needed more money for his publishing business. Leroy owed Gus a favor from years back and Gus decided to call it in. He—Leroy, that is—brings ABH Enterprises and Jack together. Jack gets a loan from Hodges, reneges on his payment or is late with the same, and . . . if Jack's fiancée is killed or harmed . . . Jack will be scared into making a quick payment. But . . . and here's the kicker, Pete, Leroy hits the boxer by mistake and pays for that mistake big time!"

"Wow!" Peter exhaled. "How will we be able to prove all this?"

John took another long swallow of his coffee before he answered.

"Vincent Parsons is going to get all of Gus's financial records, IRS records, banking, business reports of ABH Enterprises, any piece of paper at all and we'll have them examined with a fine-toothed comb. Something will fall out of the mix, I'm sure. And . . . .there's one other thing, like I said before, Tyree Embrey is missing. Hasn't been seen for days. Parsons is checking into that, too. Wouldn't surprise me to find the evil hand of Gus Hodges in *that* situation, knowing what he's capable of doing . . . to get what *he* wants."

Nineteen

Jack Davona had to admit to himself that he had made the greatest error of his life when he had trusted the wrong person.

Once, sometime back, he had read about a big television star who had advised another up-and-coming sister in the entertainment field, "Look," he reported to have said, "you manage your *own* money, girl. Don't ever put your finances in the hands of someone else."

Jack was so involved in putting out the magazine, promoting it, he'd not only given Leroy editorial freedom, which he'd approved, but had allowed Leroy to involve Gus Hodges in the company's financial dilemma. After checking Leroy's records, it became obvious that he had not made the payments to Hodges. Why? Where had the money gone? Was Leroy on Gus's payroll? Could it be that he wanted Jack to lose the company . . . to Hodges? Why would Leroy do such a thing? Jack had trusted him implicitly, had thought they both wanted the same thing—a successful publishing career.

Jack rose from his desk where he had been sitting. He walked over to his work table and surveyed the paper work, articles, photographs, items laid out for the upcoming issue of *BAD*. Was he going to lose it all?

He remembered when he'd first met Leroy at the university. He was a skinny, light-skinned kid from Vegas who couldn't understand the Boston accent and seemed uncomfortable in the urban, educational complex. He'd been glad to help the likable westerner to adjust to the city's environment.

Damn it, friggin' Leroy, dead as he was, had jerked Jack around . . . now *he* owed Hodges and what was he going to do? Money. He needed money. Money to pay Hodges—and money to keep *BAD* afloat. He was back where he'd started.

Thoughts swirled in his head. Could he sell to someone else and pay off Hodges? To whom? Could he beg Sherissa to ask her father to buy *BAD?* Could he convince her it was the right thing to do? He shook his head. She'd never agree to that. Maybe he should go directly to Mr. Holland himself.

Mr. Holland greeted Jack with a handshake and waved him to a chair beside his desk.

Andrew Holland was not a tall man, perhaps about five feet nine, but he exuded an air of authority and strength, as if he was a man not to be trifled with. When Jack presented his problem, Mr. Holland looked directly at him. "Why should *I* help you? It's my understanding that the relationship between you and my daughter ended some time ago—a circumstance that met with my approval, as I'm sure you know," he stated bluntly.

Jack ignored the barb and his face reddened with embarrassment, but he pressed his case, hoping to convince the man.

"It's a good investment, Mr. Holland. Other cities are anxious to have a similar venue in their areas. And if you, or some of your friends, could loan me some capital. . . . I'm going through a rough period right now. My editor has just been murdered."

"Heard about that. I'm very sorry. Realize you two were close."

"Thank you, we were close . . . like brothers."

In his mind Jack added, *Yeah, like brothers . . . until he stabbed me in the back, like Cain did Abel.*

He searched Andrew Holland's face for some sign of understanding, but he could not detect even a minimal trace of concern for him or his problem. And he had another nagging worry. His car had been used in both recent untoward incidents. He had not thought it at all unusual when Leroy mentioned that his own car was in the shop and asked to borrow Jack's Mercedes while he was out of town. Many times they had helped each other out in similar circumstances so the request was not at all unusual. But how could he focus on that problem when he had to concern himself with trying to save his rapidly fading dream?

Mr. Holland continued to respond to Jack's request. "I'm surprised that you allowed your company to get in such a bind. Thought, as MBA grads, you'd both have had adequate exposure to economics and money management. But as I've noticed about many young brothers, even with a college education and many advanced degrees, you all try to do too much too fast and come up with the short end of the stick. Sorry, don't mean to preach, but let this be a learning experience for you. Sorry, I can't help you."

Jack asked, "Any of your friends?" He hated to beg, and he wondered if Mr. Holland knew, or even cared, how desperate his situation was.

He watched as Sherissa's father got up from his

desk and walked to the door. "I'm afraid not. I don't wish you ill and I hope you can find help."

He offered his hand and they shook.

"Thank you, sir," Jack said. "My best to your daughter." He dared not say more because he thought if he did, his anger at having been rejected by the man's daughter would be revealed, and as disappointed as he was, he had to maintain some dignity.

The police had impounded his Mercedes, so leaving Holland's office, he slid into his rented Toyota. He drove down Route 128 from Mr. Holland's office in Waltham, hardly aware of the busy traffic moving frenetically on the highway. The frenzied roadway activity disturbed him and added to the uneasiness in his mind. He wondered if Jay had been able to come up with the names of criminal attorneys to help him with his problem. *He'd* been quite pessimistic and gave him advice that was concise and to the point the last time Jack consulted him.

"You signed the loan with ABH Enterprises against my advice," his lawyer had said. "I warned you, but you chose to trust your 'friend,' Leroy. As it is now, I'm not sure I can continue to represent you as your legal counsel. I'm afraid, son," he had said, not unkindly, "you tried to fly too high, too fast, and I'm afraid your fall is going to be a long, hard one."

A repeat of what he'd just heard from Mr. Holland, Jack thought.

Jay Treadway's dark eyes looked at Jack, noticing the undeniable anxiety that clouded the young publisher's face. At fifty-five, the veteran lawyer had experienced it all. As Jack's lawyer he had tried to steer Jack in the right direction, but stubbornly the young client thought he would succeed in his own way. He had failed.

"I'm going to lose everything, right?" Jack said.

"'Fraid so, Jack. And unless I'm wrong, you may have to do time for aiding and abetting a criminal in laundering money."

"But I didn't know that ABH Enterprises was a front for a crook!" Jack protested.

"As an educated man," the lawyer said, "you should have been aware of the Money Laundering Control Act of 1986. Money laundering is a federal crime. Your only slim, and I mean *very slim* chance of beating this is that the law does say *knowingly* helping launder money from a criminal activity—and you can claim not to have been aware of the source of Hodges's money." He shook his head. "Jack, I'm truly sorry that you got yourself into this mess and that I can't help you to get out of it. I'm not a criminal attorney, as you know, but I can recommend several good ones."

Driving along and thinking about that last meeting with his lawyer, Jack made a sudden decision to swing off Route 128 and take Route 138 through Milton and on through Roxbury. He'd head for his office in the South End and try to contact Jay. He'd get the name of a criminal attorney from him. He knew Jay was aware of his desperate situation.

As he drove up and down the Blue Hills Parkway, his thoughts turned to Sherissa. All *her* fault, he thought. If she hadn't backed out of their engagement. . . . Without thinking, he turned the Toyota onto Sherissa's street and parked in front of her condominium.

She opened the door, a surprised, puzzled look on her face.

"Jack!" Her face flushed with intense anger when she saw him. "What are you doing here? There's nothing between us, and I want you to stop harassing me!"

"Sheri, look, I'm sorry to intrude on you like this."

She did not invite him in and was taken aback when he brushed right by her.

"Jack, you have to leave! I don't want you here."

As if aware of his mistress' agitation, Zeus strolled out of the bedroom and moved between Jack and Sherissa.

Jack began to sneeze violently, one spasm after the other. "That damn cat. I hate that damn animal!"

"Not as much as he hates you. I should have paid attention to his signals long ago. Now leave!" Sherissa said bluntly.

Between sneezes. Jack persisted. "I really thought for old times' sake, for what we meant to each other that at least here I would find a kind word, a friendly face." He met her gaze, saying, "You know Leroy was found murdered."

"I'm sorry about that," she said softly.

"Know you never really liked him, and seems that you had reason to . . ."

"I never trusted him, that's all. Didn't like or dislike him, and I'm sorry he was killed." She maintained her position by the door.

Jack continued to sneeze relentlessly, his eyes became watery and his allergic reaction to Zeus became even more pronounced when, as if with malice aforethought, Zeus began to wind himself around Jack's legs and feet. He shook his legs to free himself, demanding that Sherissa, "Get this cat outta here!"

"'Fraid I can't, this is his home. *You'd* better leave." She opened the door as Jack stumbled forward, his face almost completely covered by his handkerchief as he continued to sneeze and cough.

Neither of them saw the young man standing nearby until a male voice remarked, "Hope I'm not interrupting anything."

Despite his impaired vision, Jack recognized Peter Linwood at once.

"Ah, it's you, Linwood. Come to arrest me?" Sarcasm curled in his voice.

"Not at this time, sir. But if you're ready to make a confession, I'd be happy to take you down to the precinct."

"Not in this lifetime! Outta my way, shitface," he snarled. "I'm leaving. Besides, you got nothing on me. Nothing!"

Noticing how tremulous Sherissa seemed, Peter asked her, "Are *you* all right?"

"Of course she is! Think I'm some kind of animal who'd hurt the woman I loved, will always love?" Jack spat out the words with authority as if trying to put a rational spin on the situation.

"Just go, Jack," Sherissa said. "And, please, stay out of my life."

"So you and the officer here can get it on, I guess," he said, hostile anger filling his voice.

"The young lady wants you to leave," Peter said. "I suggest you do."

"I will when I'm ready," Jack responded. "Take more than you to make me go," he said and impulsively raised his fist as if to hit Peter, who did not move a muscle.

"I wouldn't strike a police officer if I were you," Peter said firmly, his eyes firmly fixed on the angry face of Jack Davona. "I believe at the moment you have all the trouble you can handle."

Twenty

"You're not staying here," Peter told Sherissa after Jack, ranting, raving, and still sneezing from his reaction to Zeus, stormed down the stairs and out of Sherissa's condo. "He is in a bad way. Sees himself as losing it all — his friend, his business, as well as you. He's angry. The worst thing is that he puts the blame for his situation on everyone else, not where it truly belongs, on himself. I don't trust him. Got to get you away from here. Somewhere you'll be safe," Peter insisted.

Sherissa sensed that Peter was serious about her moving from her home. She shook her head, "I don't know, Peter. I feel rather sorry for him."

"Sorry!" Peter exploded. "Do you know the police are beginning to believe that *you* really were the intended victim of that hit and run? That Gus Hodges in Chicago wanted Jack to pay up, planned to take out Jack's fiancée to force Jack's hand! Leroy Hayes missed the intended target, hit the boxer instead of you, and paid for *that* mistake with his life."

Sherissa stared at Peter, horrified by what he had just said. Her eyes were wide with fear and her speech pattern revealed her increasing anxiety as she continued to question him.

"How . . . how do you know all this . . . about Jack and . . . and Leroy? And about the hit and run?"

Peter sensed her tension rising, her body temperature heating so that he smelled the soft heady perfume she wore. The fragrance tantalized his senses. She was so desirable. He couldn't bear to think that some evil person like Gus Hodges would want to harm her. He saw how visibly shaken she was and he ached to hold her in his arms to comfort her.

She sat down on her living room couch, stared at him as if to make sense of this horrendous news.

"Did . . . did you come here to . . . to tell me this?" she stuttered.

"Oh no, not at all," Peter said. "Not really. Actually, probably shouldn't have told you, but I'm worried about your safety. No, I came by just to see if you'd come back from your leave. When I drove by and saw the Toyota . . ."

"How did you know it was Jack's car?"

"We've had him under surveillance since the murder of his partner. We had already impounded his Mercedes so we knew he was driving a rental. I shouldn't be telling you this, but you must know how much I think of you and that I'm worried about your safety. Please consider staying somewhere else," he repeated. Stubbornly, she refused.

"I can take care of myself. I don't want to be run out of my own home. And I have Zeus to take care of."

"Mrs. Wallace, my landlady, would help you *and* Zeus in a heartbeat. She's a lovely lady. You'd like her. And then I'd know you were safe. My apartment is on the first floor."

"It makes me mad to be the one who has to make the changes in my life, and I haven't done *anything*. It's not fair."

Peter sensed Sherissa's strong will not to be manipulated into something she didn't want to do. He admired her for that. He knew he should back off, let her make her own decisions. Besides, because he was involved in the case, ethically it was wrong of him to become emotionally entangled. All the same, his heart was overruling his brain. He was falling in love with Sherissa Holland. He *had* to try and protect her.

Although unsettled by Jack's sudden appearance, as well as Peter's revelation about the case, Sherissa realized that whether or not she expected it she had arrived at a definite turning point in her life.

Reluctant to admit it even to herself, she was finding Peter Linwood more and more attractive. She sensed in him a sincerity and a warm concern for her welfare. Always reminded by her brother of how and what men thought about, she was disappointed by her failed relationship with Jack. And, according to what Peter had just said, she even could have lost her life. She trembled at the horrendous thought.

Peter noticed her nervousness and asked, "You all right? Can I get you something?"

Sherissa jumped up from the sofa, "No, I'm okay, but this news has been a terrific jolt to me. I'm usually calm, but this . . ." she trailed off and waved her hands in the air. "Think I'll get a cup of coffee. Would you like a cup, or something else?"

"Coffee would be fine, thanks. Black, no sugar."

She went into the tiny kitchen and Peter could hear her opening and closing cabinet doors and heard her place mugs of coffee in a microwave. The door was slammed and sounded just like his own appliance. He looked around the attractive living room with its Chinese accents and wondered if Sherissa had ever been to the Far East.

She returned carrying a tray with two steaming mugs of coffee and a plate of oatmeal cookies.

"I was just admiring the interesting Chinese artifacts you have in this room," Peter said. "Have you been to the China?"

"No, I haven't, but I hope to visit someday."

"Well, you'll enjoy it. It's a fascinating country."

Raising her eyebrows as she peered at him over the rim of her mug, she took a sip of her coffee before asking, "You've been there?"

"Yes, a friend of mine worked for a communications company and was living in Guangzhou, one of the large cities in the southern part of the country. I jumped at the chance to visit him there."

Sherissa leaned back against the sofa to watch Peter's handsome face light up as he told her about his Chinese adventure. Gone was the sober, worried look that he'd had before. She sensed that this was an experience he had really enjoyed and she relaxed, eager to listen to something vastly different from the unspeakable news she'd received earlier. She took a deep breath and settled down to listen to what Peter had to say. Funny, but now he didn't seem to be the brash, opinionated young policeman she had first met. Now he seemed to be much more amiable. He was concerned about her and was willing to share a life experience with her. She offered the plate of cookies to Peter, who declined with a shake of his head, but she took one for herself and bit into it as Peter continued to tell her about his vacation in China.

"I went in late September. Had to get a visa, which took a little over a week. I already had a valid passport and I didn't need to book a hotel because I was staying with my friend. My visa was good for up to ninety days, but I only had three weeks of vacation. I flew into Hong Kong, that's about twenty-four hours from New York, with a stopover in San Francisco."

"You crossed the international date line." Sherissa said.

"Sure did. Sunday became Monday. Funny thing, Sunday was my birthday. First time in my life I didn't have a birthday," he laughed.

"Gee, that must have been odd."

"Let me tell you, Sherissa, that was only the beginning of odd."

"The weather, what was it like?" Sherissa wanted to know.

"About what you'd find in Atlanta. Rather hot and humid."

"And the people?"

"Very nice. Friendly and respectful. I thought they would be curious about black Americans, and to a degree they were. But a number of African students study there. Most are Muslims. Arabs have traded with the Chinese for many centuries and introduced Islam to the city, which was the site of China's first mosque, so they seemed accustomed to darker-skinned people."

A sudden thought struck Sherissa, so she spoke up.

"Peter, would you let me interview you about your trip. I think it would be a fascinating piece for television: 'From Boston to Guangzhou Through the Eyes of a Boston Police Officer'. It would make a great show. I know it would. Say you'll do it," she pleaded.

"I'll have to get permission to do that. But if the brass says yes, I'd be happy to do a show with you. I was going to ask you about your job. I take it that you like it."

"I do, Peter. I like the news part, reporting current news items and breaking news events as they happen. Also, I like the special events stories like the one I'd do on you, if you can get permission."

"Understand you're a 'first'," Peter said as he helped himself to an oatmeal cookie.

Sherissa noticed him take the cookie and asked, "Would you like more coffee?"

"No thanks, I'm fine, but I still think you should consider what I said earlier."

His face, sober with deep uneasiness over her physical welfare, bothered her.

"Oh, Peter, I'm a big girl. I can take care of myself. You're like my brother . . ."

"We both care about you, don't want anything to happen."

"If it'll make you feel better, I'll think about it," she concurred.

"I hope so. You don't know what evil . . ."

Sherissa giggled. "I don't mean to laugh at what you're saying, it's just that I remember how my mother used to tell me how she and her sisters would get wickedly scared when they huddled around the radio in the evening to listen to the program *The Shadow*. 'What evil lurks in the hearts of men? The Shadow knows.'"

"Don't be fooled, Sherissa. These evil men are not shadows. They're for real!"

"I'm not making light of the situation, Peter. I want the whole mess to be over and done with."

"I'm doing all I can to help bring this matter to a close. I've got to go now. Please," he persisted, "think about finding a place to stay, at least until we sort things out."

He stood up, put his empty cup on the low table between them. He knew that he'd better leave soon before he made a fool of himself. He was fascinated by this young woman, Sherissa Holland, whom he had met in the line of duty. It was becoming increasingly difficult for him to separate his work from his interest in her. The way she had of twisting a strand of her hair around her left ear, the subtle fragrance of her perfume that enticed him, the delicate bone structure of her lovely face — it all drove him to a point to which he knew if he crossed the line, for him there would be no turning back. He struggled to keep his emotions in check, put his official policeman's face on, and strode to the door.

Sherissa stared at the closed door and thought about the man who had just walked through it. She knew deep in her heart of hearts that she wanted, needed a decent man in her life. She thought she had found what she wanted in Jack Davona. How could she have made such an error in judgment? Was there a good, kind, substantial, decent man out there? Could it be Peter? She was drawn to him, but would she make another mistake in judgment? From the first she did not like him at all . . . but now? He'd said she could still be in danger. Did she trust him enough now to believe him?

Twenty-One

"Girl, I'm so glad you called me! No point in you being alone in a time like this."

Elise helped Sherissa bring her suitcases up to her room.

"Your bed is all ready. I changed the sheets after you stayed over the last time."

"Lise, isn't it awful of me? Feel like this spare room belongs to me and Zeus."

"Awful nothin'! It's yours as long as you need it. You know that."

Elise bustled about, opening the windows to allow fresh air into the unoccupied room.

"There, that's better," she said as fresh air billowed through the sheer white curtains. "All right now, girl, give! What's goin' on in your life that you needed to seek sanctuary at Chez Daniels?" She sank down on the foot of the bed as Sherissa released Zeus from his carrier. The cat hopped right up on the bed, curled up beside Elise and allowed his mistress's friend to stroke him.

"I really don't know where to start, girlfriend. According to Peter Linwood . . ."

"You mean that fine policeman brother?"

"That's the one. He's investigating that hit and run

accident that I witnessed, and Jack's friend and partner, Leroy Hayes, was found murdered."

"Oh my God! When? Who?"

"I guess a couple of days ago. I'm not supposed to talk about this, but as my West Indian gramma would say, 'That boy Jack is in a whol' heap o' trouble.'"

"Legal trouble you mean?"

"I think so. You know, Elise, I keep wondering if there's something wrong with me," Sherissa's voice lowered to almost a whisper, "that I could have become involved with someone like Jack."

"You're not the first somebody to make a mistake, girl, and you won't be the last." Elise tried to console her friend. "I can attest to that!"

"I know, but I was so sure that I was in love with him. Now I can see through his attractive charm, his self-centered ego, he thought *he* was the most wonderful thing on earth since since sliced bread!"

"Don't be so hard on yourself, kid," Elise repeated. "That part of your life is over. Put it in the past and go on to bigger and better things."

"Like?"

"Like that brother policeman."

"You mean Peter? Funny that when I first met him, didn't like him at all. Thought he was *so* sure of himself. But now that I've gotten to know him he's caring, supportive, seems to believe in me and makes me think more highly of myself. He's very understanding. Not grandiose like I first thought."

"Well," Elise punched up a pillow and pushed it back to the head of the bed, stretched her legs out and ran her toes over the back of a contented, purring Zeus. "see what I mean? Onward and upward to a new relationship. Zeus says it's the right thing to do, don't you, man?"

"So," Sherissa continued, "that's where I am. Nice of you to let me bunk here for a few days. Peter thinks it's a good idea to have a new location. And, Elise, if you don't mind I'd just as soon not let the studio know. You understand?"

"Perfectly. My lips are sealed. I'll be as silent as our friend Zeus here."

"I'm thinking seriously, however, of getting a restraining order against Jack, just in case. Peter thinks I should."

"Sounds like a good idea to me, Sheri. A girl can't be too careful these days."

Several faxes from the Chicago police poured into John Williams's desk, and as he told Peter, "Vincent Parsons's work in Chicago has paid off."

He pulled forward a sheaf of papers explaining to his eager partner what the Chicago police had uncovered.

"They've got the evidence from Hodges's records, bank statements and more, to bring the criminal to trial for money laundering. All there in his records."

The lieutenant leaned back from his desk to watch the expression on Peter's face as he continued.

"When his money came in from his drug cartels, he used it to get into black-owned small businesses, nursing homes, daycare centers, liquor stores, funeral homes. He had lots of 'em all over. But with Leroy Hayes owing him big time, Gus found out about Davona's publishing business and he figured to launder money through that venue, especially with franchises possible in other cities around the country. Probably would have worked, too, if he hadn't turned to murder."

"Can we get him on the murders?" Peter wondered. "I suppose not, since he didn't actually commit them," he added.

"Not for committing them, but for orchestrating them. Although he had no physical involvement in carrying them out, he can be charged with aiding and abetting. And, of course, it's a federal offense to launder money."

"Of course," Peter concurred. "And if I remember my criminal law, in such cases he can be sent to federal prison for up to twenty years and be fined up to $500,000 or twice the amount laundered. Plus lose all his assets, homes, cars, furniture."

"Right. When the government gets through with him, he'll have zero, *nada*, nothing." John said.

"You got that right, and I suspect his organization may fall apart because he'll be out of circulation for some time, although he may try to keep it going from inside. The feds will keep a close eye on him. That leaves Jack Davona."

Peter shook his head. "You know, John, Davona's one strange dude. You'd think with all his smarts he'd know better than to get involved with the likes of Hodges and Leroy Hayes."

"Probably a bad judge of character. Thought everything he touched would turn to gold, because that was what he wanted. Never took the time to really understand people and their motivations. And, as I see it, the worst thing . . . he always figured he was invincible. Nothing bad would ever happen to him."

"Well," Peter agreed, "he figured wrong. He accepted dirty money to keep his business afloat, although I'm sure he's going to claim he didn't know it was dirty."

"No excuse, Pete, you know that."

"I do."

"Anyway, think we've got enough to take to the D.A. See if he wants to prosecute Jack Davona, he's the only one left of that unholy trio." He passed his empty coffee cup over to Peter, who refilled it and returned it to John.

"Thanks," he grinned up at Peter. "When I die they're going to find my blood has turned to coffee. But like I was saying, Hayes is dead and Hodges has been taken into custody. That's what Parsons's fax states."

Marshall Boyers greeted Jack with a concerned sober look on his face and led him into his ornate but dignified office. He was Boston's most well-known criminal lawyer of color, whose services did not come cheap. His office indicated as much.

"I've agreed to take your case, Jack, but I'm not sure you're going to appreciate my advice."

"And that is?" Jack said, fearing the worst.

"To plead guilty of *unknowingly* accepting money in a drug laundering scheme, and the fact that you relied on your partner, used his advise, and judgment in securing the loan . . . although you signed off on it."

"Will I have to go to jail?"

"Very likely, although I'll do my best to keep you out of it. No guarantees, you understand, but you have no priors, have been a contributing member of society. We'll have to try to work out a deal with the district attorney."

Grave disconsolation was etched in wretched lines on Jack's face as the enormity of his problem became more and more evident to him. His future was bleak. The grim notion of being sent to jail was dismal enough, but the dream of losing his publishing venture, of *BAD* going down the tubes meant that all he had tried to do, tried to attain, had lived for, would soon be nothing more than a colossal failure.

As if he could read Jack's mind, Marshall Boyers walked over to Jack's chair, placed a comforting hand on his client's shoulder.

"Needless to say, I am sorry about your predicament, but I think I have found a legitimate buyer for your business."

"You have?" Jack asked, a small glimmer of hope in his eyes.

"Yes. You know my services don't come cheap, so I went ahead, set out some trial balloons, and there is some genuine interest if you wish, that is, to sell."

Jack shook his head. "What alternative do I have?" he mumbled, his head lowered into his hands.

"None that I can think of. So, as I see it, Jack, there are three things you want me to do. Post bail to keep you out of jail, try to plea bargain with the D.A., and unload your company. Right?"

Overwhelmed by the gravity of his situation, Jack could hardly speak. He nodded his head in assent, shook his lawyer's hand and left the office, his shoulder slumped in dejection. It was the worst day of his life.

Twenty-Two

Kendra Williams flew down the stairs to stand in front of her father who was waiting in their living room to accompany her to the Celtics opening game.

"Ta-dah!" She bubbled over, twirling around so that her father could get a good look at her outfit. "How do I look, Dad?"

Her face glowed with eager anticipation as she waited for his response.

"Like a million!" he beamed. "Sure your old dad is good enough to take out a beauty queen like you?" he smiled.

He thought she looked great, as usual, in her denim overalls, black turtlenecked shirt, and carrying a red cardigan sweater in case the night turned chilly. Her black hair, done in narrow braids, was tied back with a red silk scarf. Her father was pleased to notice the tiny diamond studs in her ears that he and her mother had given her for her birthday. Kendra, his only child, was the apple of his eye and he didn't care that folks said he overindulged her. "It's my great pleasure to so do," he would say.

As for Kendra, she adored her father. She always tried to please him, be the son he did not have. She knew her father loved basketball, so she tried out for basketball and made the high school team. To attend the Celtics' opening game was a treat she looked forward to sharing with her father. As they walked out to the car parked in the driveway, Kendra asked, "Dad, you think the Celtics will play Elijah Kotambigi tonight?"

"The new recruit from Africa? Gee, honey, don't know. Would be something to see, though, wouldn't it?" he said, smiling at her obvious excitement.

They had very good seats, partly because John Williams was a season ticket holder and partly because he was a Boston policeman. Crowds of people were streaming into the Fleet Center, their faces glowing with enthusiasm and excitement, looking forward to the opening game of the new season.

Kendra turned to her father after they had settled in their seats. "Isn't this exciting, Dad?"

He looked at her exuberant face and grinned. "It sure is, honey, sure is."

As he looked over his daughter's head, his grin faded quickly because he saw the face of someone he recognized. It was Hector Ransom, the late Nate Gamble's boxing trainer. He was sitting almost crammed in by two overly large men. Both men were well-dressed and well-groomed. John Williams remembered them from the cemetery at the boxer's gravesite. He wondered, *Now what did these three people have in common?* Then he remembered something. Hector Ransom, a.k.a. Frank Nicholas, had been a mule, a runner for Augustus Bell Hodges back in Las Vegas. Was that connection still viable? He'd have to look into that fact. It meant maybe an entirely new development in the case, he mused. He thrust the idea to the back of his mind to enjoy the basketball game with his daughter. His wife, Helen, frequently reminded him, "Make the most of these times you spend with your child because they'll soon be gone and you'll only have these treasured times to re-member." As usual, Helen was right. Kendra was growing up so fast and soon there would be no time for Pops, as she sometimes called him. The business of Hector Ransom would have to wait for now.

"Look, Dad!" Kendra squeezed her father's arm. "There he is!"

The sports announcer's voice boomed over the loud speaker as he introduced, "Number eleven, our newest recruit, playing center position, Elijah Kotambigi! Give him a Celtics welcome!" The crowd's boisterous cheers and applause for the new recruit were loud and sustained. The young African acknowledged the welcome with a wide smile, pumping his raised fist into the air in a responsive salute.

WHAB's television studio had been arranged to resemble an attractive living room. Two large comfortable chairs were situated behind a black-lacquered coffee table. On it a luxurious red amaryllis plant rose majestically from its bed of waxy green leaves. In the center it was flanked by a black and gold ceramic jar with a cover that made it look like a miniature pagoda. On the other side a single yellow chrysanthemum floated in a bowl of clear water.

The show's producer, an attractive young woman, perhaps a few years older than Sherissa, Peter guessed, welcomed him when he arrived at the studio.

"Welcome, Officer Linwood. I'm Rebecca Greenwood. It's very nice to meet you and to have you as our guest."

"Thank you, Miss . . . Greenwood. I'm pleased to be here."

She walked beside him down a dimly lit corridor,

explaining that some were on-air broadcast studios and others were settings for various programs. He spotted television cameras and equipment as they passed opened studios and in other rooms he saw banks of television screens, computers, and recording equipment.

"Right here," Ms. Greenwood said and she led him into the room set aside for the program.

Peter had been cleared by the police department to do the interview, but since he was on his own time, and this interview was not official, he wore civilian clothes.

Sherissa was seated at one of two chairs and raised her head when Peter entered with Rebecca Greenwood, her producer.

Her heart lurched wildly in her chest when she saw him. She thought he looked quite handsome. He wore a mauve shirt with a tie of the same warm rose tone, and his suit was a crisp steel gray. His hair appeared to have been freshly cut and lay neat and trim against his head.

His face was wreathed in a warm, friendly smile. Directed to the empty chair by the producer, he leaned over Sherissa to place a light kiss on her cheek before he sat down. "So glad to see you. How are you?"

"Fine. Just fine," she responded in a matter-of-fact tone. She hoped her tentative smile did not reveal the unexpected nervous anxiety she felt. *Calm yourself, girl*, she said to herself. *What's wrong with you? He's not the first interview you've ever done. Get hold of yourself. Be professional! Just get on with it.*

Peter thought Sherissa looked quite professional and stunningly beautiful. She seemed poised and composed, ready for the interview to take place.

Who am I kidding? he thought. *Why would a lovely, talented young woman like Sherissa Holland want to be bothered with an ordinary, mule-headed, dumb policeman like me?*

A cranberry-red silk blouse with a soft cowl-like neckline framed her face and brought shimmering highlights to her hair. She wore a silver chain belt which accented her small waist. A slim black leather skirt that ended at her knees and the sheer black stockings that covered her shapely legs completed the portrait of a well-groomed sophisticated upwardly mobile young black woman.

The theme music for Sherissa's program, *The City and Its People,* rose in the background and on the monitor Peter saw Boston's skyline, a view of Trinity Church, the Charles River Esplanade, Old South Church, Fenway Park, and Fanuil Hall all arranged in a moving montage. The old city looked good to him and he felt an unmistakable swell of pride that he was part of it. The studio lights came up and since Peter had been told which camera to focus on, he looked in that direction and saw his own image. Sherissa's voice came through.

"Good evening. I am very pleased to have as my guest tonight on *The City and Its People* one of Boston's finest. Detective Sergeant Peter Linwood was a recent visitor to China, to Guangzhou to be exact, a large city in southeastern China, a port city like our own Boston."

She turned to face her guest and began to question him.

"Sergeant Linwood, how did you happen to visit China?"

He answered promptly. "A friend who was working there invited me. I had vacation time coming, so I decided to take him up on his invitation. I'm glad I did."

"Did you like it?"

"Let's say it was an enlightening experience," he smiled.

"How so?"

"For one thing, it is an ancient civilization many, many centuries older than ours."

"And the people?"

"My friend, Luke," Peter explained, "works for a world-wide communications system, so most of the people I met were his colleagues. Almost all of them had received some education here in the States so they were familiar with us and our customs. However, I did have the pleasure of having dinner with one of Luke's close friends and his family."

"At their home?" Sherissa wanted to know.

"No they arranged for Luke and me to meet them one evening at the Guangzhou Restaurant. It was something else! The food was excellent. We even had abalone sprinkled with flakes of what looked like gold. Lamb, goose, beef, it was a fabulous meal, and we were treated like royalty."

"The city itself, what was that like?"

"Well, it's an old city that began as part of the Silk Road where merchants took caravans south to send their silk, jade, spices, sandalwood, and other luxury items to trade with ancient Rome and the Arabs. Believe it or not, during the 7th century Islam was brought to China and the first mosque was built in Guangzhou. Facts like that really opened my eyes."

"Are there modern parts to the city?"

Peter nodded his head and smiled at Sherissa, who had relaxed and seemed to be enjoying the interview and smiled back at him. There was no tension between them and they appeared to be two friends sharing a friendly discussion.

Peter reached for the glass of water on the low table, took a sip before he answered.

"You've asked the question most everyone wants to know. And the answer is yes, because it is a port city and close to Hong Kong, it has become a very modern city. There are high-rise apartment buildings, skyscrapers, new highways, and shopping centers."

"How long was your visit, Sergeant?"

"Not long enough. There was so much to see. Markets, museums, temples, even the Tomb of the Kings containing the remains of the king and his staff who were buried with him to care for him in the afterlife."

"That must have been something to see" Sherissa said as she leaned forward to refill Peter's glass of water from the carafe on the table. She was fascinated by this new aspect of Peter, his ability to share so eagerly his unusual experience with her and her television audience.

She asked him, "How did the people there react to you as a black American?"

"Some of them were curious, but there have always been people of color in China—Arabs, Indians, and Africans—because of the ancient trade routes. The Chinese that I met were mainly interested in trying out their English. I understand that English is required in the schools."

"And how about you? Did you learn any Chinese?"

Peter laughed. "Very, very little. '*Nee how*' is hello and '*nee how mah*' is how are you? Speaking phonetically, that is. I'm not that good with languages," he confessed. "Don't seem to have the ear for it, but perhaps if I had stayed longer, I would've learned more. My friend Luke does fairly well with the language, but he's been there several years."

"Would you like to go back?"

Peter nodded. "Yes, I would. It's a large country with a large population. I only visited a small area, but yes, I'd like to go back someday."

As she listened to Peter talk, Sherissa realized that perhaps her perceptions of him were wrong. He didn't look like a stereotypical police officer, act like one nor talk like one. What was wrong with her to pre-judge a man before she even knew him? She had been wrong about Jack Davona, too, she admitted to herself.

She found herself staring at Peter Linwood's hands. Strong, supple, graceful, they seemed capable, able to handle whatever was expected. She wondered how those hands would feel if he touched her. How would she react? She brought her mind back to the present to hear her guest saying, "I did not identify myself as a police officer because I was not visiting in an official capacity and, besides, the government's policy on human rights differs from ours."

"I expect that was wise thinking."

"That's why I did it. Better to keep silent," he smiled.

Sherissa faced the camera and made a closing state-ment to conclude the interview as the strains of the theme music rose and the screen dissolved into the station's call letters.

"You were great!" Sherissa told Peter as they re-moved their mike buttons hidden beneath their collars.

"It was my pleasure. Anytime you want to interview me, I'm available," he smiled.

She walked to the front lobby with him and Peter was reluctant to leave. He knew he had to speak of what had been bothering him.

The front of the lobby was a wall of floor-to-ceiling

windows and the sunlight streaming through them cast light and warmth throughout the area. Seating arrangements of comfortable chairs, low tables with potted ferns along with pamphlets about the television station were inviting settings for intimate conversations. With a nod of his head Peter suggested that they sit down. Sherissa followed Peter, instantly aware that Peter had something more personal on his mind.

He cleared his throat, looked about the almost empty lobby. Occasionally someone walked through, but he and Sherissa were seated in a corner of the room away from the traffic so he felt he could say what was on his mind.

He saw Sherissa's eyebrows raise inquisitively as she waited for him to speak. She had rested her left arm on the arm of her chair and began what to him seemed an endearing habit of twisting a strand of hair. *Oh God, help me make this right. Don't let me goof up.*

"Look," he started, leaning toward Sherissa, "I know that when we first met I came off as an arrogant, know-it-all, smartass. I know I did and I want you to know that I'm very sorry and I apologize for such stupid behavior. Somehow I had the need to try to impress you. What a jerk!" he slapped his hand against his forehead.

Sherissa smiled. "I wouldn't go so far as to say that. You're not a jerk."

"What would you say?"

"Well, I don't mean to sound egotistical but I'm flattered that you did want to impress me . . . . even though I was a bit irritated."

"You're very kind and I don't deserve such consideration." He leaned forward again to take her hand. It felt right to touch her at that moment, and she accepted with a response from her hand in his.

"I'm sure you're aware that the police code of ethics frowns on officers becoming too closely involved with persons that may be a part of an investigation . . ."

"You're not concerned about losing your own career?"

"Yeah, my partner warned me all about the impropriety of even *thinking* about a relationship with you and I've been reluctant to contact you on a social basis, but . . ."

"What has changed? What made you decide to ignore his warning? Aren't you afraid of losing your job?"

"As much as I love my work—and I do—I'd have to give it up if it came to that. I can't, I won't let it come between us."

This time he took both her hands in his. They were soft and warm. He rubbed his thumb over her knuckles and she heard the deep sincerity in his voice that seemed to emanate from the very core of him.

"Sherissa, I'm very attracted to you in spite of my inadequate, overbearing, stupid approach when I first met you. I want to know you better. I'm begging you to give me a second chance, a new beginning."

While Peter was explaining his position, Sherissa couldn't help but think of her failed relationship with Jack. She had been so captivated, so enthralled by being loved by a worldly, sophisticated media mogul like Jack. Could she, should she even consider starting a new relationship? She knew what her family would say, but she was a big girl now and it was high time she began to make her own decisions and stick with them. Peter's open-faced, straightforward approach appealed to her. She made up her mind.

"You've been honest with me, Peter, and I appreciate that. I don't want you to mess up your career because of me, and, besides that, I've got to be truthful, as well.

I can't begin to consider a new relationship, not until I can figure some things out . . ."

"I know," he interrupted. "I understand that you're freeing yourself from your past engagement. I certainly do not want to pressure you, not for a moment. Only want to make you aware of my feelings, that's all."

Then his tone of voice became more serious. His eyes never left hers. "I want to be sure you are safe. You have my beeper number, don't you?"

"Yes, I still have it."

"Good. Can we start over on a new note?"

"What do you mean?"

"Will you have dinner with me? Tonight?"

"Would it be okay with your lieutenant? Aren't you investigating . . . ?"

"I'm not investigating you. Only had to ask you questions as an eyewitness. The lieutenant knows of my interest in getting to know you. We won't say it's a date," he suggested, 'just continuing my interview."

Twenty-Three

They went to a seafood restaurant near the harbor. They had a window table which allowed them to see planes land and take off from Logan Airport. They settled into their seats and Peter took a look around, pleased that the restaurant was not overly crowded. It was quiet, conducive to intimate conversation and privacy.

Sherissa wore a black and white geometric print sheath dress with black spaghetti straps and over her shoulders she had draped a black silk brocaded shawl. Large, gold, hoop earrings accented her short haircut which curled sleekly over her ears. Peter felt his heart beat in triple time as he looked across the table at her. He prayed that the evening would go well and put him on the path that would lead him to what he knew he wanted—a successful relationship with this lovely, exciting woman.

Sherissa was glad that she had accepted the detective's invitation. After today's interview she realized that Peter Linwood was more than just an ordinary cop. She knew that it took courage and strength of self to admit to one's mistakes or weaknesses. She admired Peter for his ability to do that and his character rose in her estimation. He was very well groomed. Tonight he wore a black suit with a white silk turtleneck shirt. When he picked her up in his car she noticed he was wearing black socks with black tassel loafers. She thought he looked quite elegant and she found herself very comfortable and at ease with him. Would this man be in her future?

The waiter handed each a menu, a heavily embossed, large, folded affair with a silk cord and tassel down the centerfold. The entrees listed included many fresh seafood offerings plus steak, lamb, veal and chicken, each prepared specially for the restaurant's discerning clientele.

Peter watched Sherissa as she looked over the menu. He could hardly believe his good fortune. There was a subtle sophistication about her, an elegance, an air of grace and propriety which attracted him. On the other hand, there was her sense of delight in living that made him ache to insure her happiness. He could barely keep his admiration of her to himself.

Her large luminous eyes, stunning cheekbones and her sensuous mouth intrigued him and he had to speak. He leaned toward her.

"Before the waiter comes back to take our orders, I have to tell you how lovely you look tonight and that every man in this restaurant is jealous because *I* am in the company of the most beautiful woman on the planet!"

She shook her head and laughed.

"Sure you don't have some Irish blood in you? Or have you kissed the Blarney Stone recently?"

"Negative and negative to answer both questions, my lady. I speak only the truth, and you know as a police officer I'm required to do so."

She laid the menu on the table and shook her head at him again.

"Still think you got that clever gift of a quick tongue from somewhere."

"Well, it could be that a bit off the 'old sod' touched my family. My mother, God rest her soul, was Helen Flaherty, born in Barbados. I really don't remember much about her because she died when I was four."

Sherissa frowned. "How awful. I'm so sorry. Your father?"

"From what I've been told he took my mother's death really hard. He allowed me to be legally adopted by my maternal grandparents and they raised me here. My father went to Alaska to work on the pipeline and he died there."

"All of that must have been hard on you growing up," Sherissa suggested.

"I suppose it would have been, but you see, I was greatly loved and protected by my grandparents and they saw to it that I got a good start. My mother was their only child so I was very special to them."

The waiter came at that moment to take their orders.

"Have you decided what you'd like?" Peter asked Sherissa.

"I'd like the lobster casserole," she told him. "I love lobster but don't want to mess with it."

"Wise choice," the waiter smiled at her, waiting for Peter's decision.

"Make mine the sea and surf, with the steak medium. And for our salads, how about a Greek salad with plenty of Feta cheese?" he asked Sherissa.

"All right by me," she agreed.

"Wine, sir?" the waiter asked Peter.

"Oh yes, a bottle of your house red wine, please."

"Certainly, sir."

"How did you happen to get into police work?" Sherissa returned to their conversation.

"My granddad worked for the post office. He was a sorter at the South Postal Annex. He'd been educated to be a teacher back on the island but couldn't pursue that here in the States, you know. Anyway, he did all right as a postal employee . . . sent me to college. Didn't know what I wanted to do and after I got my degree, still didn't know." He broke off. "Sure you want to hear all this?"

"Of course," she said brightly.

"Well, okay then. My granddad said 'Whatever you do, try to get a job with some benefits.' But I couldn't seem to find what I wanted and just by chance decided to take the police exam. I passed that, was accepted at the police academy and graduated. Worked the beat for a while, then I went back to school, got a master's in criminal justice, got promoted to sergeant and assigned to the detective squad, homicide division. That's it."

"And you like your work?"

"I do. It's more than just policing. It's trying to right a wrong, bring a measure of justice to the victim and his or her family. I believe that detective work makes one use all sorts of thinking, to concentrate on the mind of the perpetrator, to pull pieces of evidence together, to answer the why and who-done-its. To me it's very rewarding."

"You plan to stay in police work?"

"Think so. I'll be taking the lieutenant's exam soon and then see what happens."

He looked up, saw the waiter approaching with their salads and a bottle of wine. "A-ha, food's here!"

"Would you like the wine opened now, sir?" the waiter asked.

"Later I think, when you serve our entrees," Peter said.

"Very good, sir." He placed the bottle in a wine holder. "Enjoy your meal."

"Now, let's hear about you. Every detail, leave nothing out," he said as he popped a black olive in his mouth.

"Salads look delicious" Sherissa said. "Let me see," she began. "Born and bred right here in Boston. Went to Boston Latin . . ."

"Oh, a brain, eh?" Peter teased.

"Don't think so. I have a twin brother, you know, so it was competition all the way. And I resisted my family's attempt to always try to protect me. So I studied hard. Felt I had to. After I graduated from college I knew I wanted to be in journalism, and when the opportunity came, the offer from WHAB, I auditioned and got the job."

"I'm sure there's more than what you've just outlined, but I can be very patient and wait to hear the rest of the story," he said. "That means we get to spend more time together. Right?" He raised his eyebrows, waiting for her response.

"Hm-m-m, maybe," she smiled.

"That's what I want to hear." He pumped his fist into the air, a wide grin on his face.

The food was excellent, well-served, and the complex flavors of the wine added to the elegant meal. Background music that filtered softly into the dining area only added to the seductive ambiance that increased Peter's hopes for a successful evening with Sherissa. He wanted desperately to touch her, get close to her, hold her, convince her of just how precious she had become to him. However, he knew he could not rush her. She had only recently freed herself from her relationship with Jack Davona and Peter was certain she was wary of any new alliance. He had to tread lightly. *One step at a time* he reminded himself. Hopefully tonight would be a step in the right direction.

Their food arrived hot, and as Sherissa remarked, "I always like having my food served at the right temperatures, hot foods hot and cold foods cold. It shows the chef knows what he or she is doing."

"I agree," Peter said as he started to eat. "How's your lobster?"

"Perfect. I'm glad you brought me here. It's very nice," she said, looking around.

The decor was nautical, without being overdone. The restaurant was on the water and large windows offered an excellent view of the Atlantic Ocean. As she looked out of the window near their table, she could see the roiling ocean waves as the tide neared the beach. A full moon cast a glowing path over the cresting waves and she was glad that she could see the glorious wood fire that burned in a huge fieldstone fireplace on the opposite wall. A feeling of serenity and peace came over her and she repeated what she had said earlier. "It's very nice. Very nice."

Dessert was a spectacular concoction, a house special that appealed to the couple. The waiter described it to Sherissa.

"Ma'am, it's a thin-shelled delicate meringue shaped like a small boat filled with fresh vanilla ice cream and topped with crushed strawberries and whipped cream."

"I'd like that. How about you, Peter?"

"Yes, indeed. Sounds too good to pass up. And black coffee, please. Two."

Sated by their meal and relaxed with each other, Sherissa and Peter were quiet on the drive to Roxbury and her condo. Peter felt that so far the evening had been a success. They had explored each other's background and felt comfortable with the resulting disclosures. Sherissa had even declared that she saw Peter's work as a noble profession. That insight coming from her pleased him. *What a woman,* he thought.

Driving through the night in Peter's car, Sherissa wondered to herself how the night would end. She and Peter had talked tonight as if they had known each other for years. The conversation flowed freely and easily between them, with Peter enjoying her stories of growing up with a twin brother.

"I think most of the time," she had said, laughing at the memory, "Todd thought *he* was my parent, always looking out for me, protecting me . . . too much of *that,* really."

Sitting in the darkened car she sensed she had reached a crossroad in her life. She made up her mind just as Peter pulled the car up to her condo.

"Would you like to come in for more coffee?"

"That would be very nice," Peter answered.

They walked up the sidewalk to the front steps and Sherissa handed Peter her key. He opened the door and they each entered the vestibule. Peter closed the door and they went up to the second floor to Sherissa 's condo. Each knew their relationship had moved to a new level with Sherissa's invitation and Peter's acceptance.

A few days later Peter drove Sherissa out to Cambridge to meet his grandparents.

"My folks are anxious to meet you," he explained, "and I think Gram is going to have dessert and coffee for us when we get there. She fussed at me because she said she would have had high tea, but I didn't give her enough notice."

"High tea? What's that? Sounds real formal."

"Well, yes, I guess it is. It's the Bajun legacy from the British. You know, delicate cucumber and watercress sandwiches, petit fours, crackers, chutneys, one's best table linen and china, all that stuff. My Gram loves all that fancy English formality. She was raised on that."

Peter's grandmother reached for Sherissa with open arms.

"My dear, 'tis a welcome sight for these old eyes to meet you."

She was a small, nut-brown woman with quick movements, and when she smiled up at Sherissa, her eyes crinkled warmly at the corners and her smile revealed the most attractive dimples in her cheeks that Sherissa had ever seen.

Peter's grandfather watched over his wife's shoulder as the two women greeted each other and he reached forward to give his grandson's friend a warm hug when his wife turned to him.

"Look, Warren, this is Peter's friend. Isn't she lovely?"

"Indeed, indeed, that she is. Welcome to our home, my dear."

Sherissa saw at once that Warren Flaherty had passed his handsome good looks to his grandson, Peter. Except for Peter being taller and Mr. Flaherty a little grayer, they were almost identical. Sherissa thought, *This is how Peter will look as he ages. Slender, dignified, and warm.* The older gentleman enveloped her in a warm hug.

"Peter has told us so much about you, and I must say, my dear, that you are lovelier in person than on television. Right, Peter?"

"You are all very kind," Sherissa murmured, and there was no doubt in her mind, she felt a quiet serenity come over her. She was not among strangers. Not at all.

Twenty-Four

Elijah's agent informed the young player that the Celtics management had agreed that he could be interviewed by Sherissa Holland for her television program, *The City and It's People.*

"Of course, you're not to talk about player-management affairs," he warned Elijah. "Just general comments about how you're adjusting to pro basketball, your own goals, what you think of the city and the fans . . . that sort of thing, you know."

"I understand," Elijah said.

"Good. I've already briefed Miss Holland and she understands, too. Enjoy your interview."

On the scheduled day, following the directions given him by his agent, Elijah made his way to the WHAB television station. It was not quite 9 A.M. As he got out of the taxi, he looked up at the building he was about to enter. He'd been told there could be a possibility that he could get a tape of today's interview to send to his parents. He reminded himself to ask if such a thing could be possible. His folks would be so proud and pleased. It would give them a chance to see and hear their son who'd been away from home for over five years.

He paid the taxi driver and was about to walk up the short flight of stairs into the main lobby when he heard a commotion a few yards away to his right. He turned in time to see a man wearing a black ski mask force a woman into the back seat of a black Volvo. She was protesting, resisting the man's attempts by kicking and flailing her arms.

"Stop! Stop! Leave me alone!" the woman screamed. "No! Get away! No! Nooo!"

"In the car, bitch!" Elijah heard the man growl. Elijah stared at the action, not certain if he should intervene. Something made him start to run after the car when, with tires squealing, it careened around the corner out of sight. But not before Elijah saw the woman turn her head, look out the back window, her eyes wide, pleading for help.

Elijah recognized her! Miss Holland! Galvanized into action, he raced into the lobby, confronted a startled guard who had not expected a six-foot-ten-inch black man to come in shouting, "Miss Holland, Miss Holland's just been kidnapped! Just now! Right outside! She's gone!"

"Hey, hey, calm down. What're you talkin' 'bout? She jes' left to go joggin'."

"It's the truth, sir. She didn't want to get into the car but the man with the black mask pushed her. Made her get in. She looked out the back window, she saw me. I know she did. I know it was her!" Elijah panted, horrified by what he had just witnessed.

"Okay, okay, who're you?"

"Elijah Kotambigi. She was to interview me."

"Ah, yes, the Celtics player."

"Shouldn't we call the police, do something?" Elijah pleaded. "There were two men. A fat one, the driver, and a skinny one who pushed her into the car. I think the license plate was like," he closed his eyes to remember what he had seen, "let me see. Yes, yes, H-H-460. Green and white."

"New Hampshire. We'd better call it in," the guard said as he reached for the phone on his desk to call 911.

The morning after their date Peter went to the station feeling pleased that his time with Sherissa had gone well. It was almost as if each of them had been determined to forget the past and start anew.

He was glad that he knew how to reach her at her new address. At last she showed a little confidence in him. And she had given him her pager number, as well.

He couldn't help it, though. His stomach churned with apprehension whenever he thought about her. He had a gut feeling that all was not as it should be. It was a 'waiting for the other shoe to drop' feeling that kept bothering him.

Lieutenant Williams was at his desk with the inevitable cup of coffee when Peter sat down at his desk across from his superior.

"Well, how did the television interview go?"

"Good. I think Miss Holland was pleased. At least she said she was. And she did tell me that she took my suggestion and has moved in temporarily with a friend."

"That so?"

"Yes. She indicated that her former fiancé, Jack Davona, had been calling frequently, can't seem to realize that the relationship is over."

"That's too bad. She shouldn't have to be pestered like that. And," the lieutenant added, "I'd think with what the charge of money laundering he'd have enough to worry about."

"Maybe he thinks she can help him with his money problems. Her dad is well off, you know."

"So I've heard."

"Well, did he make bail? Is he out of jail?" Peter asked.

"D.A. says so. Took out a lien on his publishing business. Expects to sell it, I believe."

The telephone rang.

"Williams here."

As he listened to the message, the lieutenant stood up and motioned to Peter that this call was urgent. Recognizing the look on the lieutenant's face, Peter grabbed his coat as the lieutenant jammed down the receiver.

"Miss Holland's been kidnapped!"

Less than five minutes later they were at the television station asking questions, seeking answers.

Mr. Osgood, the station manager, thought they should make a breaking news announcement that one of their own had been kidnapped. The police agreed and the bulletin went out with no mention of the hit and run incident that had previously taken place at the same site.

After they had questioned Elijah, the guard and everyone else who had spoken to Sherissa that day, they returned to the precinct office.

The lieutenant was driving. He sensed how upset Peter was feeling.

"Somehow, John, in my deepest gut I was fearful of Sherissa's safety. And now this!" He slammed his fist on the dashboard. "I'll never forgive myself if anything happens to her."

"Can't think like that, son. Think positively."

"I'm trying, but it's hard."

"Listen to me, Pete. This is one of those times when

you have to put your personal feelings aside and think like a policeman. By the way," he added, "didn't the basketball player describe the driver as on the heavy side and the guy hassling Miss Holland as thin and wirey?"

"That's how he described them."

"Think, Peter, about this cast of characters that we've been dealing with on this case."

"If you start with the hit and run victim, Nate Gamble, then Leroy, also killed by a . . ."

"Then," John prompted, "who ties those two together? Think, man!" he said as he pulled up in front of the precinct station.

Peter frowned for a moment, then his eyes widened as a name came into his mind. "Hector Ransom! He was the boxer's trainer and he knew Leroy from back in Las Vegas!"

"And the head honcho . . ."

"A.B. Hodges!"

"Right. And I wouldn't be surprised if he's not behind this kidnapping plot."

"But why?" Peter wanted to know. "From what the Chicago police said, he's sitting tight as one of Uncle Sam's house guests, isn't he?"

"Something you have to understand about the criminal mind, Pete," John said as they walked into their office. "Don't know if they covered this in Psych 101, but contrary to thought, a seasoned career criminal like Hodges is not dumb. Not at all. He just uses his brain to work against the law. He's clever, manipulates people to get what he wants. Even if he's six feet *under* the jail, with fear and intimidation he can still control those who work for him."

"Same as some of the mob, I guess."

"Right. And I think I spotted Hector Ransom the

other night when my daughter and I were at the Celtics game. He was sitting between two heavyset goons and I remembered we'd seen them at the boxer's funeral."

"You're kidding? I remember them, and also that their car had New Hampshire plates."

"We'll ask the New Hampshire police to run that plate through their DMV and see what they come up with."

"And I think," Peter added thoughtfully, "it's time to check out Hector Ransom's gym."

On the evening news that night, WHAB reported as its lead story the kidnapping of one of its staff and offered a reward of $10,000 for information leading to her safe return.

A close-up of Sherissa Holland remained on the screen with the station's telephone number. In addition, the police headquarters number scrolled below.

Twenty-Five

Terrified, Sherissa's overwhelming fear threatened to choke off every breath she tried to take. She was going to die! Her chest felt tight, constricted. She could only scream and kick at the back of the front seat where her two black-hooded abductors sat. The driver was a fat, seemingly middle-aged man, and the one who'd pushed her into the back seat was a thin man, but he seemed very fit and strong. She had been no match for his power when she had tried to fight him off.

It was he who turned to face her. Both men's faces were hidden by the balaclavas they wore, but this man's eyes revealed harsh, deep anger directed at her.

"Shut up, bitch, an' stick your hands out!" he demanded. Seeing a gun in his hand, she complied. Horrified, she watched him hand the gun to the driver who continued to drive with one hand while the thin man taped her wrists together with heavy duct tape.

"Now," he ordered, "sit still." He proceeded to tie a silk scarf over her eyes, around her head, and wound more duct tape over the scarf.

"Okay, we can take care of business now," he said to the driver who only grunted in response.

Oh God, what business? Sherissa wondered as she

sank back into the corner of the back seat. *Who were these men and what did they want with her?*

She tried to take stock of her situation. Had Elijah, the basketball player, recognized her? She thought about Peter who had said how worried he was about her, even indicating that maybe someone was even out to kill her. Why would he think such a thing? Was that what these men planned?

She was wearing only sweats, white socks, and her running shoes. In her left pants pocket she had a small purse with some change, a dollar or so, and in her right pants pocket her phone pager. Would anyone find her? Was anyone looking . . . like, maybe, Peter?

Sitting with her head against the back seat she tried to visualize the route the kidnappers might be taking. She remembered the sharp right the car had turned into and she recalled seeing a red light when they had stopped on the avenue. After that she was blindfolded and could only guess that they were on a route that would take them out of the city.

"Glad to take that damn thing off my face," she heard the driver say. "Fuckin' thing nearly choked me, fuckin' hot! Whew! Turn on the air conditioner. Get some air in here!" he said.

"Better than havin' the chick see your ugly puss! No more talkin'," the thin man ordered. "Jes' drive."

He did not turn on the air conditioner, merely opened the window on his side and the driver did likewise, breathing deeply. Sherissa heard whooshing sounds as cars passed by, then she began to notice that the sound of cars seemed to decrease. She smelled a change in the air. She could detect the salty air of the ocean and a noticeable chilliness. They hadn't been driving long enough to have reached the north shore, but maybe Revere, Winthrop, or Nantasket. Then she heard it, a plane. Winthrop, she guessed, they were somewhere near Logan Airport. She thought it was interesting how, deprived of her sight, she was already relying on other senses to help her.

"Turn here," she heard the thin man's voice order the driver. When the car stopped, he got out and she heard him open the back seat door.

"Okay, girlie, out!"

She shrank from his touch as he grabbed her elbow and pulled her out of the car. She felt sand beneath her feet as her captor led her, pushed her when she stumbled blindly, attempting to secure her footing.

"Up two steps, now," the man directed. She heard him put a key in a lock, then open a door as he pushed her inside. He made her walk through what she thought might have been a kitchen from the odor of a gas stove and the distinct hum of a refrigerator. Her feet moved over a smooth surface, tile or linoleum, and then she heard another door being opened and she felt a rush of cool air. She was being taken to a basement of some sort. It must have been turned into a family room now because there was carpeting on the stairs and on the floor. She was led to a couch, turned and pushed to a sitting position.

"Wait here," the kidnapper demanded.

Sherissa heard him leave, run up the carpeted stairs. She listened intently but could hear only muffled voices. Who were these men? Why had they kidnapped her?

She tried to wiggle her hands to see if she could loosen the tape, but it was many layers and very tight. She continued to struggle, trying to flex and move her hands to release some of the tension of the duct tape. She stopped, sat very still when she heard returning footsteps.

"Now," the man said, "I'm tellin' you how it's goin' down." His voice was hoarse and gruff as if he'd been yelling and screaming at a football game or some other sports venue. The truth was he'd been coaching a new young boxer who had raw talent but was proving hard to train.

"I'm takin' off the blindfold, gonna untie your hands. You're stayin' right down here in this family room. There's a bathroom you kin use, but you gonna be locked up down here. No way you kin git out. There's a bed you kin rest on . . . okay?"

Sherissa nodded. She felt the man's hands on her head, and with unexpected gentleness he cut the bindings at the back of her head. Released from the bandages that had covered her eyes, she blinked several times as she tried to focus and check out the man who stood in front of her. She stared at him.

He wore the black balaclava and a black leather vest over a ragged white T-shirt. He had on dark blue jeans and white sneakers. She could see that his arms were well muscled, and although he was thin, he appeared to be very fit and strong. To her fearful horror, Sherissa thought he looked like an executioner. His dark eyes bore into hers as he continued to talk.

"I'm takin' the tape off your hands, but you betta' behave or by Jesus you'll be sorry! You're to do as you're tole' an' that's it. Unnerstan'?"

Sherissa nodded again as she flexed and clenched her freed hands.

"Why have you brought me here? Who are you and what do you want? I don't know you!"

"But, lady, I know you," the main said, sarcasm dripping from his tone of voice. "I know who you are and that's why you're here. You owe me! Now shut up!"

He walked over to the foot of the staircase and picked up a cell phone.

"Call your father. I'm sure you know how to reach him. When you get him on the line, I'll take over. Go ahead, call him, an' no shittin' me aroun'. Do exactly what I say." He glared at her through the sinister slits around his eyes.

From her previous reporting experiences, interviews with victims, interactions and seeking information from people in unusual circumstances, Sherissa knew that her best chance out of her predicament was to be co-operative and patient. She forced herself to be calm, not allow her frayed nerves to show as she dialed the phone.

"Yes, Dad, it's me. I'm okay . . ."

The man quickly snatched the phone out of her hand.

"Yo! Listen up! I want a hundred thousand by six P.M. tonight." He glanced at his watch. "Eleven-thirty now, got plenty of time. Small bills, deliver to a locker at American Airlines. I'll call back, you'll tell me the number an' combination of the locker. No fuckin' police or your *daughter* is fuckin' history!" He slammed the receiver down.

He clumped up the stairs after admonishing Sherissa that she'd better cooperate, taking the cell phone with him.

After he left she heard the door at the top of the stairs being locked. Sighing deeply, she decided to check out her surroundings. She found the bathroom. It was clean and well stocked. There was a shower with a glass door, and a small electric coffee pot on the lavatory counter. The bed was full sized with clean linen and had a soft blanket folded at the foot. Sherissa's heart leaped when she saw on the back wall french doors leading to a patio, but she knew the doors would be locked. She tried them and they were. They were sheathed in black plastic so she couldn't see outside.

She went back to the bathroom and after using the facilities, washed her face and hands with warm water and soap, a fresh cake that she unwrapped. She heard the door open at the top of the stairs and then close again and locked. She walked to the foot of the stairs. On the top step she spotted a small tray of food. Well, at least they didn't intend to starve her.

All of her life she had been protected by her family. Today, this moment, she knew she had to fend for herself. Her life depended on whatever skills, talents, judgment, or intuition she could summon if she were to survive. She was alone and she was on her own.

She was too nervous to be hungry. She had to think. *Think, girl, calm yourself Think back!* It was about nine this morning when she set out for her jog. And she was returning about three quarters of an hour later when she was accosted. After being pushed into the car she remembered that she was sitting in the back seat on the passenger side of the car and the sun was warm on her right side. Could that mean she was being driven north? North, out of Boston? She recalled a sense of being near the ocean and . . . of hearing planes. Where had she been taken? And most of all, why had she been kidnapped? The hooded man said he knew who she was and that she owed him. Did Jack have anything to do with this? Did he hate her *that* much?

Twenty-Six

Lieutenant Williams spelled it out to Peter and the rest of the staff.

"We have two fronts we have to work on. We have to find Sherissa Holland before she comes to harm, and we have to find out who took her."

Everyone in the room agreed that the kidnapping of a television person had to be solved. It took first priority.

"The state's attorney's office is already involved and we've put out an all-points bulletin for the location of the car, which we now know was stolen from Hampton Beach in New Hampshire. It's a Volvo. The state police are on the lookout for it and its occupants. The television people are offering a reward and Miss Holland's picture will be shown. Also," the lieutenant continued, "the other thing is, the community wants to help."

The phone rang and all eyes were on Lieutenant Willams's face when he picked up the receiver. The silence was thick with everyone's heart-chilling anxiety.

"Yes, Lieutenant Williams here. Yes, I see. We'll have a team at your place in ten minutes, sir. I understand, I understand perfectly, sir. Right away. Yes, indeed."

He replaced the receiver and briefed his eager fellow officers.

"That call was from Mr. Andrew Holland, Sherissa Holland's father. He's just received a call from her kidnapper demanding money."

There was a collective inhalation from each one in the squad room, followed quickly by questions. Who? Where?

The lieutenant lowered his hands on his desk to quell their inquiries.

"Yancey," he said to one of the men, "I want you and Winston to go to Mr. Holland's office to set up a tape to record the next call when it comes in. Mr. Holland said he was advised by the perp not to call the police or his daughter would be harmed. So, you'll have to go in undercover."

"Window cleaners?" Yancey, a young clean-cut detective asked.

"Yes. All-Right Cleaners, Inc."

"We'll get on it right away."

"And don't forget your window-washing coveralls! Let me know as soon as you get anything. Here's the address."

Mr. Holland's computer business and office was located off Route 128 in Waltham and within minutes after the telephone call Yancey and Winston were on their way, dressed as window washers, in a truck equipped with monitoring devices.

Peter's anxiety level was so overwhelming he thought surely everyone in the room must sense it. Was it only two nights ago that he had taken Sherissa out to dinner with a promise to see each other again soon?

He'd asked her that night, "Is everything okay with you? No bothersome phone calls?"

"Like I told you," she'd said to him, "I'm staying with my friend."

"Good idea, but remember, I'm only a phone call away."

"Why don't I give you my phone and pager number," she'd remarked. "You might get a lead on a hot story and I'd be very happy to be the first reporter on the scene."

Now his guilt was weighing him down. He should have insisted that she move to Mrs. Wallace's house where he lived. But how would that have helped? She worked every day and so did he. As it was, she was snatched right off the street first thing in the morning. Why and by whom? They had to find her. No, *he* had to find her.

He waited for the lieutenant's next assignment.

The Chief of Detectives, Captain Muldonney, strolled in, handed Lt. Williams a sheet of paper. The two men had a few words, and after the captain left, the lieutenant beckoned to Peter.

"The girl's father wants to offer a reward, too, but the captain thinks we should hold off making an announcement until we check out a few more leads."

"I see. So what are we goin' to check out?"

"You remember that we had a sheet on the boxer's trainer, Hector Ransom, a.k.a. Frank Nicholas, who was a mule in Las Vegas for Hodges?"

"I recall that, yes. What about him?"

"It's time to check *him* out. Come on!"

"Lead the way!" Peter said, anxious to see some action.

The man they met at Hector Ransom's gym didn't know where his boss was. In fact, Hector had not planned to be in that day, he said, after the police showed their badges. The place was fairly quiet with a few young wannabees sparring with each other in a corner ring while a middle-aged man looked on, making appropriate comments as warranted.

"Does your boss drive a black Volvo?" Lieutenant Williams asked the man who seemed to be in charge.

"Nah, he don't drive. Lost his license sometime back. Folks drive him, or he takes a taxi."

"Does he have a friend who drives a Volvo?"

"Could be. Hector got lotta friends."

"But you don't know."

"Ain't really up on cars that much, 'specially them foreign ones."

The lieutenant nodded. "So," he prodded, "you don't expect Mr. Ransom to show up later today?"

"Like I said, I don't 'spect so, but if he do come in?"

"Give us a call, or have *him* call, ok?" Peter handed the man a card.

"Yes, sir, officer."

Peter joined the lieutenant in the car, feeling very discouraged that they had not been able to contact Hector Ransom to question him.

"I think we ought to keep a close watch anyway on the activity at the gym," Williams said. "I know how anxious you are to find a solid lead, but something will turn up. And, son," he looked over at Peter's worried face, "I know Miss Holland is starting to be special to you."

"What are we going to do? I just can't sit around."

"For now, nothing. When the kidnapper calls back . . ."

Suddenly Peter banged his fist on the dashboard and the lieutenant stared at him.

"What? What?"

"Call back, you said! Lieutenant, I've got her beeper number! I can try to reach her!"

"Wait, wait, let's think this thing through. We don't want to jeopardize her safety or alert her captors."

"But, John . . ."

"When we can get back to the station, we'll talk about it. Need to evaluate everything. We're dealing with desperate men who don't think twice about doing desperate things."

When they got back to their desks, Peter explained.

"See, lieutenant, this is a newer type wireless phone. It's small," he let the detective feel the weight of the phone. "Weighs about six ounces and has a standard battery. Now, on this instrument I can receive and/or send messages and I don't have to speak into the phone. I can display my message here," he pointed to a blank space which showed the time and had the word menu printed on it."

"How will Miss Holland know you're calling her. That is, if she has the phone with her?"

"She told me that she always carries it because she never knows when she may be called for a breaking news story."

"Suppose her phone rings, won't the kidnappers hear it? My wife and daughter have these phones and they ring."

"No, because she *always* keeps it on the silent mode so if she's at a meeting a ringing phone won't disrupt anything. See, there's an optional vibrating battery. If it's in her pocket and she feels the vibration, then she can look at the menu and see the number of whoever is calling her. It's displayed right there!" Peter pointed excitedly at the tiny screen.

"So, let me get this straight. You punch in her number, type in your message and send it."

"Right."

"And no one else will get this message?"

"No one else," Peter said emphatically.

His face was flushed with excitement as he punched Sherissa's pager number.

Sherissa sat on the bed which was farthest away from the staircase. What was going to happen to her? Would her father call the police despite the kidnapper's warning not to do so? Would he be able to pay the ransom? And why had she been taken? Had Peter been right all along, that someone wanted her dead?

She threw herself back on the bed, buried her face in the pillow and that's when she felt a distinct vibration in her sweatpants pocket. Her beeper! *Someone* was trying to reach her! She was *not* alone. She read the message on the menu. WRU? *Where are you?* she deciphered. And below the message was Peter's pager number. Thank God, she breathed, that her captors had not searched her and found the beeper.

She flushed with excitement as she read Peter's inquiry, WRU? *He's asking me where I am, but I don't know!* She typed the message, *DUNO,* don't know.

Peter whooped when he read her answer.

"Lieutenant, we've reached her! Look at this! Now she knows we're searching!" He punched his fist into the air.

"Good, good. Ask her for directions to her location."

"Okay. Let me think. *TLMDIR,*" Peter printed out.

Tell me directions, but there was no answer. He stared at the phone in his hand. Nothing.

"We'll have to give her time. Be patient. We don't know what's happening and we have to give her time to think." John tried to sound encouraging.

Peter sat, his chin resting on his two hands as he stared at the phone, willing it to react. He thought he would go out of his mind. When he could stand it no longer, he got himself a cup of coffee as if he wasn't already nervous enough. He sat down, waited for the coffee to cool when suddenly the phone began to vibrate.

AMSUSHINRTSH. Peter read the letters out loud to John.

"Am sushi? Does she mean she's near fish?"

"I don't think so, John. Remember I asked for directions. I think *AM* is morning and *SUSHIN* is sunshine. *RT* means right and *SH* means shoulder.

"So, she's saying, let me think, morning sun on my right, which means, Peter, that she was traveling north. We better alert the state police north of Boston and have them look for the car. I think this may be the break we need," John said.

"Sherissa is a very bright person. She's level-headed, and I know she's going to be able to figure something out," Peter figured.

Within a few minutes Sherissa lived up to Peter's expectations. A new message came through. *Planes ocean apt.*

Peter wondered. He showed John the message, up to fifteen characters, the most that could be displayed on one line. But below that was another message, *Basement.*

"She's someplace north of Boston, near the ocean,

in the flight path of planes in and out of Logan and she's in the basement," John figured.

"How many towns are north of Boston near the ocean and in Logan's flight path?" Peter wondered.

"Get back on that thing and ask her how long a drive it was. That'll tell us about how many miles she may have traveled and then we can concentrate on that area."

Twenty-Seven

At about four that afternoon a call came into the precinct that instantly galvanized both Peter and John into action.

From the limited communication between Peter and Sherissa, he and John were able to determine that it was most likely that Sherissa was being held in or around Revere. She had indicated that her blindfolded ride had taken about forty-five minutes, and when Peter asked if she thought she had traveled through the Callahan Tunnel she said she thought so. In addition, she indicated smells of fresh paint and new carpeting in the basement made her think the building she was in was new. A townhouse, perhaps, because she could hear car doors slamming, footsteps thundering down staircases which made her believe she might be in the basement of a condominium.

Armed with this information, Peter put in a call to Revere City Hall's building department to check for the location of any new housing construction near the ocean, also in Logan Airport's flight path. They promised to fax that information as soon as possible.

But it was the news from the Massachusetts State Police that made the two detectives rush out of the police station and into the squad car. The stolen Volvo had been located. The state police found the missing vehicle parked near Revere Beach, right in front of a concession stand whose logo above the wooden open air stand purported to have *The best Ipswich fried clams in town*.

Peter drove this time, using the siren and lights to get through the early afternoon traffic.

"I hope they've got an eyeball on it so they can tail whoever drives that car," he said to John.

"Said they put an unmarked car on watch," John told him. "And if the call comes in to Mr. Holland from the perp, and we're able to trace it, we should be able to wrap this thing up, especially if the Volvo leads us to where they're holding Miss Holland."

Peter maneuvered the police car expertly through the traffic, aware of his increasing tension and anxiety. All he could visualize was Sherissa's lovely face and he prayed silently that no harm had come to her.

Hector Ransom was obsessed. He was angry. He'd been cheated out of reaching his goal by others. But, by damn, he was going to get what was rightfully his— or die trying. The girl was the answer. With the hundred thousand from the girl's father he could fade into obscurity on one of the small islands in the West Indies. He'd told no one about his eye problem, but the doctor had already said he would soon lose his eyesight. As a boxer, he had been hit too many times in his eyes. There wasn't much time left if he was going to enjoy any life at all. He had to act, and act fast.

Two weeks ago Gus Hodges's orders to kill Sherissa Holland to light a fire under Jack Davona had failed. Hector had passed the assignment to Leroy Hayes, who knew he still owed Gus and that he'd better get rid of the girl. Leroy had been forwarding Jack's payments to Hodges Enterprises as ordered, but the plan was Gus would deny having received them. Thus, by Jack's default, Hodges would own *BAD* and be able to continue his money laundering scheme. But Leroy had failed.

"What the fuck could I do?" he protested to Hector when he had to admit he'd killed the wrong victim.

"It was so dark, rainin', foggy, an' the guy was right in front, like you said! I thought it was the girl!" Leroy admitted to Hector who could hardly control his anger at the inept behavior of the young man whose worried expression and sweaty face revealed his anxiety. Leroy knew how important Nate Gamble had been to Hector, who saw his boxer's win as a way to move into the prime time. Even the promoter, Don King, had shown interest. Now that opportunity was gone and Leroy was very concerned about his own future.

He needn't have worried because Hector had plans for him. It had all been easy and quite simple. He called Leroy.

"Yo, Leroy! Yeah, it's me, Hector."

"Hey, Hector, my man," Leroy tried to sound normal and jocular as if all was well between him and Hector, adding, "What's up?"

"Nuthin' much. Same old same old, but lissen' up. The boss has a job he wants you to do."

"Even after I messed up? Jeez, not like Gus to forgive a mistake."

"I know, I know, but he said he understood. It bein' dark an all. Said that's water over the dam."

"I owe Gus big time and you can bet my life I won't mess up this time! Glad to have a chance to prove myself," Leroy said, his voice rising, anxious to redeem himself.

"Okay, here's the deal. Meet me at Franklin Park at four tomorrow morning. Bring Davona's Mercedes, he's got it back from the police impound, I checked it out. Gus still wants to tighten the screws on Jack. Park near the field house. I'll be there an' I'll fill you in on the details. Okay?"

"Sure thing. No problemo. I'll be there. Lucky Gus still believes in me."

"Yeah, right. Gus knows you're a loyal soldier from way back in Vegas days."

Hector hung up. He sat at his desk in the corner of the now quiet gym, thinking. Leroy and Jack Davona were the educated ones. Yet they still had allowed themselves to be seduced and tainted by Gus Hodges and his money.

And who was he? Only a half-Mexican kid who'd found his way to limited success by honing his natural boxing skills. Mr. A.B. was the one who told him to go into training boxers after his eye problems began. He had owed Mr. A.B. for a long time since he'd been a mule transporting drugs for him. Happily, his ability to train successful boxers pleased Mr. A.B. As for himself, his time was running out, but still he owed Mr. A.B. He hoped this last assignment would clear the slate. He ached for a life of serenity and peace. He'd find that at his island retreat. He could hardly wait, but he had to deal with Leroy first.

Leroy was right on time. Hector stepped out of the shadows of the field house just as Leroy drove up in Jack Davona's quiet Mercedes.

The two men greeted each other with high fives

and Hector got into the passenger's side and told Leroy to drive along the outer perimeter of the golf course.

"You know, Leroy, the feds are holding Gus."

"Yeah? How come?"

"They got hold of some of his records, accusing him of money launderin'. Something like that. But he's still runnin' the show. You know Gus. Turn right here," he told Leroy, indicating a less-traveled roadway. Leroy did so and Hector told him to stop the car. Leroy did as he was told. They got out of the car and Hector turned to his companion.

"Leroy, wait here for a minute, will ya? Ever since the doctor put me on medication for my blood pressure, seems like I got to take a leak every time I turn around. Be right back."

He scurried around the trunk of a huge oak tree and sighed deeply and loud enough for Leroy to hear him.

"Feel better?" Leroy asked. He had not heard the light-footed Hector creep up behind him, but he stiffened when he felt the cold steel of a gun at the back of his head.

"Much better," Hector said, and he fired.

He pushed Leroy's body until it rolled down the grassy slope to come to rest at the foot of the hill. Then he got into the car and drove slowly through the Blue Hills Reservation. He saw poorly with his damaged eyes, but the white center line led him through the winding streets up the Big Blue until he came to the Boy Scout summer campsite. Luckily there was no traffic at that hour. He turned the car into the drive until he reached a blocking barrier and could go no farther. Satisfied that the car would not be spotted easily from the road, he wiped the steering wheel, the dashboard and the inside of both windows and removed the keys. Then he wiped the door handles and both the driver and passenger side. Tossing the car keys into the woods, he walked to the street, Chickatawbut Road, until he recognized the spot he was searching for. He took a small flashlight out of his pocket and beamed it over the area until he spotted something. Pushing the brush aside, he righted a bicycle, pushed it out to the road and rode to his apartment located in Mattapan, not far from the reservation. The whole episode had taken about an hour.

Twenty-Eight

Peter managed to drive through the Callahan Tunnel just ahead of the early evening rush hour traffic.

"Always a slowdown at Bell Circle, the rotary," John reminded him.

"I know," Peter agreed, "but if there's no racing today at the track, we may get past that area with no problems."

At that moment their police radio crackled. John Williams picked up the receiver. The Revere police informed him that the car being watched was moving and was being followed. John radioed back to the Revere police that their estimated time of arrival was five minutes.

"You're telling the dispatcher that our ETA is five minutes? You know where we're going?" Peter asked John.

"Sure do," John grinned at his young partner. "Spent many a day and night when I was a teenager at Revere Beach and I *do* know where the police station is. Trust me," he laughed.

Peter's tension eased a bit as he concentrated on driving through the maddening traffic. He recognized John's attempt to try to keep him focused on reality. He knew as well as anything else that to be encumbered with inner turmoil and anxiety could very

well get in the way of clear thinking. Of all the part-
ners he could have been paired with, he was lucky to
have been teamed up with a seasoned, no nonsense,
experienced one like John. And he was grateful for
that.

Sherissa was too nervous to eat the bagel and cream
cheese that was on the tray. She didn't like bagels, anyway, and she wasn't at all certain about drinking the
coffee. Who knew what could be in it? She settled for
some water from the bathroom faucet. Then, restless
and agitated, she sat down on the couch. Were the police going to find her? Peter's communication with
her had encouraged her, but she glanced at her
watch, it was almost five. Had her father called the police? Would he get the money? Had Peter been able
to locate this place? Then she heard the key being
turned and the door unlocked. She reached into her
pants pocket. The pager! She had left it on the bathroom sink! She rushed into the bathroom, slammed
the door shut before Hector reached the bottom stair.

"Come on out! We're leavin' here!" he yelled at her.

"Be right out," Sherissa said as she flushed the toi-
let to make him think she'd been there for a while.

"Hurry up! Ain't got all day!"

When she came out slowly, a hooded Hector
grabbed her, tied her hands behind her back with a
thick cord and tied a scarf over her eyes. He led her
up the stairs where he threw something, a blanket she
thought, over her head and bustled her out to a car.
It didn't seem to be the same car as before, had a
newer smell, and as they drove off it seemed to be a
lighter weight than the previous vehicle. Where were
they taking her now? The car seemed to be slowing

down at times, then speeding up at other times, and once she heard Hector's gravely voice complain about the "fuckin' traffic." Finally she became aware of the smell of exhaust fumes and the muffled sounds of cars. They were in the tunnel! Heading back to Boston! But where to?

The next radio call that John and Peter received was from the Revere Police. *Have Volvo driver in custody. No sign of victim.*

When he and John pulled up to the new condo in the Oak Hill section, the police were interrogating a neighbor. Peter was beside himself. He asked the neighbor, a middle-aged man who told him, "Haven't lived here long, only moved in last month. Don't know many of my neighbors."

"But what did you *see?* You told the Revere police you saw someone being put into a car, you say?" Peter asked, anxious to get to the core of the matter.

"That's what I said, Officer. I didn't know if someone was sick or something, the person was so wrapped up in a blanket, couldn't see the face."

"Man or woman?" John asked, his pad and pencil in his hand to make notes.

"Couldn't tell you that. Could have been a young boy or a girl. I could see from the legs, sweatpants, gray, I remember, and white sneakers. Sorry, that's about it."

"The car?" Peter prodded.

"A kinda new blue Dodge. Intrepid, I think it was."

"Thanks very much for your help," John told the man. "If you think of anything else, here's my card."

He and Peter thundered down the front steps of the neighbor's condominium and as soon as they got into the car John radioed the Boston police to be on the lookout for a blue Dodge Intrepid that might be coming through the tunnel. The Revere police were already on the alert.

John headed back the way they had come, upset and disappointed that they had probably missed Sherissa and her abductor by a few minutes according to the neighbor's time frame. If they'd only been there ten minutes earlier . . .

This time the traffic had slowed considerably. Cars jockied from four lanes of traffic into two lanes leading through the tunnel under Boston Harbor from East Boston to the city.

"I hate traffic!" Peter complained, "especially in this damn tunnel."

"Know what you mean," John said. "This is one of those times when you have to be patient. Can move only when the cars in front of you move, and once you get into a lane, have to stay there. No crossing the center line," John said. He glanced over to the right lane which appeared to be moving faster than the lane they were in. Then he did a double take as he noticed a shiny blue car move past. As he did so, his mind on the neighbor's comments, he checked for the car's style name. There it was, *Intrepid. Dodge Intrepid.* He looked at the license plate, a Massachusetts plate, number NA984.

"Peter, Look! I think that's the car! We've got it. Careful now, don't make a move on it! I'll call it in to the boys. They'll pick 'em up when they come through the tunnel."

However, Hector had spotted the police car with the plainclothes detectives inside. He told the driver, "Keep your speed and watch out. There's cops two car lengths behind us on the left."

"Wha ya wan' me to do?" the driver asked.

"Head down the southeast expressway as soon as we're out of the tunnel! We'll ditch the car . . . place I know . . ."

"The broad?" the driver asked.

Sherissa trembled when she heard Hector mutter, "There's always the quarry."

The Quincy quarry? Where so many bodies and stolen cars have been dumped? But wasn't the quarry filled up with soil removed from the Big Dig, the project that was taking so long and so much money to complete? Or was there another quarry someplace else? Girl, you've got to do something! Can't let your life end like this!

During the ride the car had careened around a corner, throwing Sherissa off balance and she lay prone on the back seat. Luckily the two men in the front seat were too busy with the traffic to concern themselves with her. With the thick blanket over her head she was able to rub against the heavier material to dislodge the silk scarf Hector had tied around her eyes. He was in such a hurry this time he had not used duct tape. Now the silk scarf hung loosely around her neck. If only she could free her hands. Was she doomed to die before she ever had a chance to experience real love? Especially now that she believed she may have found it with Peter Linwood? Would she ever again see the concern in his eyes that made her know he cared?

The car sped down the expressway, over some temporary steel plates that had been placed over construction sites, and the bumps and jolts of the car threw Sherissa to the floor. She grunted, but the men did not hear her. Then she heard it, a police car siren.

"Floor it! Fuckin' cops!" Hector demanded.

Responding to the urgency of the police, other drivers moved off the road. All but the Dodge Intrepid.

It careened madly down the expressway, narrowly missing slower traffic.

As Sherissa struggled to free her hands from the heavy rope tied at her wrists she heard Hector yell, "Watch out for that Fed Ex truck!"

She heard a whoosh as the car sped past the large truck. Then she heard Hector's next instructions.

"Take the next right!"

She felt the car swerve and she sensed the vehicle was being driven up a very steep incline because, laying on the floor, her body was pressed back against the bottom of the seat. She continued to struggle, trying to pull her right hand through the rope at her wrists. She could feel her skin being abraded by the rough texture of the rope, but she gritted her teeth and kept trying. She tried to pull her hands apart in a fashion that would allow the fingers of her left hand to pick at the knots of the rope, but she had little success. Frustrated, she kept pulling both hands, trying to free them despite the searing pain. She knew her hands were raw and bleeding but she continued rubbing, pulling, picking at the restraints. The sounds of the sirens were getting closer when suddenly the car stopped and she was yanked out of the car. Rough hands pulled the blanket close and Hector's voice chilled her. "Here's the end for you, girlie!"

She heard men's voices. "Police! Stop right there, Ransom! Put both hands up!"

She was pulled, dragged, felt large stones beneath her feet as she tried to squirm out of her captor's grasp, but he was strong and her efforts only angered him. And she felt a gun at her back.

"Let the girl go, Ransom!"

Peter! It was Peter's voice!

"She's goin' over the side!"

"You don't wanna do that, Ransom! We know you killed Leroy Hayes. Found the car keys hangin' on a tree branch up in the Blue Hills where you threw 'em, and found your thumb print on 'em. You're in enough trouble, don't make it worse!"

"He made a mistake, offed my boy . . ."

Peter's voice sounded authoritative as he persisted. "Don't make it worse for yourself. Let . . . the . . . girl . . . go!" he demanded.

Then it all happened. As Ransom pushed her, guns were fired almost simultaneously. Sherissa screamed when her feet left the ground. She felt her body fly through the air and the loose blanket sailed free from her body. Then she knew nothing more.

Twenty-Nine

Peter rushed over to the police car, opened the trunk to retrieve a coil of rope.

"Oughta wait for the fire department and EMTs," John advised as he saw Peter secure a length of the rope around his waist.

"You know I can't do that, John. Got to go!"

"I understand." He beckoned to a nearby officer. "Pete's goin' to rappel down to check on the victim. Tie the end of the rope to that tree," he pointed to a sturdy oak, "and stand by to help."

Several other police had arrived and had taken Hector Ransom's driver, who could be heard protesting his innocence, into custody. "Only drivin' the car, that's all," he continued, even while being advised of his rights.

The ill-fated Hector lay dead under a plastic sheet while the police waited for the medical examiner. It was a scene of controlled chaos as Peter rappelled his way gingerly down the inside of the quarry partially filled with dirt.

"Don't move her," John warned as he watched Peter's slow progress. "The paramedics are on their way. Med-Evac helicopter, too!"

Peter's heart raced with fear for Sherissa as he reached the hard-packed soil about thirty feet down.

She lay crumpled up in a fetal position. Her eyes were closed, but she was breathing.

"Oh, Sherissa, honey," Peter murmured as he reached for her wrist. Her skin was warm and dry, and when he took her pulse it seemed strong and steady. He winced when he saw the bruises and torn, abraded skin on her hands. Quickly he cut the rope, but mindful of the lieutenant's admonition, he did not move her arms.

"She's been knocked out!" he yelled to the police looking down. "Breathing okay, I think."

Then he heard the rotor engines of a helicopter overhead. Within minutes that seemed like an eternity to Peter, two emergency medical technicians were lowered to Sherissa's side. Immediately they checked her vital signs and declared them stable. They checked for signs of injury and noticed that her left foot lay at an awkward angle.

"May be fractured," one of the medics said, and he proceeded to apply a splint. When he did so, Sherissa moaned but did not open her eyes. "Responds to pain," the other team member noted.

As soon as they could do so, moving quickly and efficiently, they secured their patient to a portable litter and signaled for her to be hoisted into the helicopter. Within seconds she was being transported to the Boston Medical Center.

Peter's first thought was to go to the hospital, but John dissuaded him.

"Later, Peter. We still have plenty of mopping up to do right here at this scene. Her family has already been notified, the doctors have been advised to let us know when she regains consciousness. I've put a police guard on duty, so we have to wrap up this Hector Ransom business."

"He's dead?" Peter asked.

"When he pushed the girl, we saw the gun."

"Yeah, I saw it, too. Think he was aiming at me . . ."

"Who knows who he was aiming at? When told to drop the gun, he refused. Several officers fired and that was it. He got it. Found his gun, a Glock, nine millimeter. Same gun that killed Leroy Hayes."

"And the driver?"

"He's in custody. Says he was only driving Ransom around, didn't know nothing 'bout *no* kidnappin'."

"He's an accessory. He'll do time," Peter said.

"That's for sure," John agreed. Then he added, "He's got a yellow sheet, too. Prior convictions, so he won't be going anywhere soon."

The doctor's reports were better than Peter had expected. Sherissa's left ankle had been fractured, she had suffered a mild concussion which had caused a temporary black out, and she had multiple bruises and abrasions on both hands.

Peter impatiently strummed his fingers on his kitchen counter as he stood by his wall telephone waiting to be connected to Sherissa's hospital room. He had called every day to check on her condition. Usually the nurse or whoever answered gave him very little information when he identified himself as a friend: "in fair condition" or "vital signs within normal limits."

"Sherissa Holland, please," he said when someone said hello.

"Speaking," a soft, quiet voice responded.

"Sheri!" Peter yelled into the phone. "Is that you? How *are* you? How're you feeling?"

"I'm doing okay. This you, Peter?"

"Yes, yes. It's me! When can I come to see you?"

"Anytime," she said softly. "But . . . I'm going home tomorrow."

"To your apartment? Your friend's?"

"No. To my folk's place. The doctors think I may need some help for awhile and my folks insist that I come home. They want to take care of me."

"Don't blame them. They've been through an awful lot."

"Guess so."

"So, may I come visit at your folk's place?"

"Of course!" Peter noticed that Sherissa's voice sounded much stronger than when she'd first answered the telephone.

"I'll give you the phone number," she added, "so that I can look presentable."

"Are you kidding! Girl, you'll always look good to me!" Peter was happy when he heard Sherissa giggle at his remark.

"I look forward to seeing you, Peter, and before I forget, thanks so much for the flowers you sent. They are lovely."

"My pleasure, believe me, my pleasure."

The Holland residence was located in an affluent suburb of Boston and Peter was not at all surprised when he drove into the driveway and parked his car behind a new Lexus.

Sherissa's father greeted him at the front door with a welcoming smile.

"Come in, come in! It's so wonderful to meet you, Detective Linwood. Sherissa's spoken so highly of you."

"How is she?"

"Doing great! Almost back to normal, I'm happy to say. Come right this way," and he led Peter through a beautifully decorated living room and a dining room with a table set for a meal, lunch maybe, Peter thought. They passed through the dining room to a sun-filled solarium nicely appointed with rattan furniture. Sherissa was lying on a chaise lounge with her left leg in a cast. Crutches rested nearby where she could reach them.

"Peter! So good to see you." She extended both hands to him and he grasped them, leaning forward to kiss her forehead.

He was dismayed to see the remaining discolorations and bruises on her face and arms. But her smile was radiant and she seemed glad to see him.

An extremely attractive middle-aged woman came into the room at that moment and Peter recognized at once that she had to be Mrs. Holland. She looked so much like her daughter they could have been taken for sisters. Only her hair, cut in the same short pixie-like haircut as Sherissa's, was a soft, becoming gray.

Peter moved quickly from Sherissa's side to greet her mother.

"You must be Sherissa's mother."

"Detective Linwood, welcome! It's a pleasure to meet you." She reached up to give him a warm hug, and as she did so she murmured into his ear, her voice sober from her deeply felt emotions at meeting the man who helped save her daughter from a fate too horrible to imagine, "Thank you. I can *never, ever* repay you."

Peter responded, shaking his head as he stepped back, "No thanks necessary. Only doing what I have been trained to do. But I'll admit to you," he smiled and looked over at Sherissa, "your daughter has become very, very important to me, and I had really strong motivation to try to rescue her. And, please, call me Peter."

Thirty

Sherissa insisted on walking to the dining room, using her crutches.

"You know, they wouldn't release me from the hospital until I could show that I could ambulate with these things. Even taught me how to go up and down stairs."

As Peter suspected, Mrs. Holland had prepared a lunch.

"Very nice to have a home-cooked meal," he complimented his hostess.

She served him an ample helping of lobster salad, sliced tomatoes, cucumbers, and small rolls.

"There's plenty more in the kitchen, so eat all you want," she told him as he raised his hand in a gesture of restraint.

"Everything's wonderful, I'm fine, thanks."

Mr. Holland refilled Peter's wine glass with chilled wine. He placed the carafe near Peter's place setting.

"Now, son, you just help yourself. As my mother used to say when we sometimes had company for dinner when I was growing up, 'Help yourself to anything you see and anything you don't see, we'll show you how to get along without it.'"

Peter laughed, feeling relaxed and accepted by Sherissa's folks.

"Detective . . . er, Peter," Mr. Holland's voice grew serious as he helped himself to a roll from the basket on the table, "what can you tell us, or are you not allowed to talk about our daughter's ordeal?"

"The investigation is still in progress, but evidently there is a link between Sherissa's kidnapper and a drug dealer out in Chicago. Both Ransom, the kidnapper, and Leroy Hayes, the man he killed, were involved in drug dealing in Las Vegas years back. Both Ransom and Hayes were controlled by Augustus Bell Hodges, the drug boss."

"But," Sherissa wanted to know, "how did Jack get involved?"

"I believe he trusted Leroy."

"Yes, I guess so. He worked so hard to make *BAD* successful. He was willing to leave the financial part of it to Leroy."

"Who," Peter interrupted, "was being controlled by Hodges, who in turn wanted *BAD* as a vehicle for his money laundering."

"Why did Ransom murder Leroy Hayes? He had nothing to do with it," Mr. Holland asked.

"Hayes evidently botched Hodges's order, I'm sorry to say, to kill your daughter in an effort to force Jack into believing he owed money to Hodges, although Hayes and Hodges were keeping the real truth from Jack. The money was being paid by Hayes. Anyway," Peter continued, "Hayes made a mistake and killed Nate Gamble, the boxer who was out jogging that morning. Gamble was up for the middleweight title and Ransom had plans for bigger and better things. He was planning to strike it rich."

"What a mess!" Mr. Holland said. "So, he was angry enough, or crazy enough, to take a man's life?"

"Right. He knew he had to, on Hodges's orders. He kidnapped your daughter as his last chance to get ahold of some big money that he felt he'd been cheated out of."

"Oh," Mrs Holland said, "let's not talk about this any more! It's too upsetting."

"It is," Peter agreed, "but Sherissa, I'm happy to say, did her part. It was a good thing she had her beeper and was able to communicate with us."

"I was scared to death but I knew I had to do what I could. Thank God you detectives figured everything out. Peter, what's going to happen to Jack?"

"I really don't know. Understand he has a very high-priced lawyer. He may try to cop a plea that he was unaware that he was aiding and abetting a person, meaning Hodges, in a criminal act."

"Poor Jack," Sherissa murmured.

"Poor Jack nothing!" her father said. "I believe the only reason he sought you out in the first place was because he thought, through you, Sheri, he'd have access to my money for his publishing business. Do you know even after you two broke up he came to me for money?"

"He did?" Mrs. Holland asked.

"Yes, he did. Of course I turned him down. And then he wanted to know if any of my friends would be interested. He was a disappointed man when he left my office, let me tell you."

Mrs. Holland cleared the table and brought in dessert and coffee.

"I hope you like apple pie," she said to Peter.

"My favorite," he smiled as he accepted a generous slice with a wedge of cheddar cheese.

They took their coffee back to the solarium.

Sherissa declined Peter's offer of assistance with

her crutches. "I can manage myself," she told him, "I'm going back to the station part-time."

"You are? Are you ready? What does the doctor say?" he questioned anxiously.

"He agrees part-time is just fine. I plan right now to do my interviews, *The City and It's People.* As a matter-of-fact, I'll be doing the interview I never got to do with Elijah Kotambigi. You know, the Celtics new recruit."

"That's right! He's the one who witnessed your abduction." Peter shook his head. "Thank God that's behind us now. And I'm glad the doctor has cleared you for part-time work. I know how much it means to you. When's your cast coming off?"

"Dr. Frier said a couple of weeks."

"Good. We'll celebrate. I'll take you out to dinner."

"I'll look forward to it, Peter."

Lucky "Doc" Reynolds got the call that night at eleven. He'd just started cleaning the ladies' restroom at the Ford car dealership where he worked every night.

"Yes, Boss, it's me." He listened to the brief message, replied. "Yes, consider it done."

Doc was not surprised to hear from the man who'd helped him get his present job. Working at night, cleaning up the showroom, offices, and lavatories was a cinch and gave him his days off to go to the track. But he owed Mr. A.B. Guessed he always would. Tomorrow he'd have to do some checking, find out what he needed to know about his target. Mr. A.B. had said his trial date was set for next month and the hit had to be carried out before then.

The next day Doc made his rounds, checked out the newly remodeled police station, noticed the number of cars in the parking lot, the entrances and exits around the station house and then he drove off.

A few days later, in mid-afternoon, when he knew the duty roster would be changing shifts, he went inside up to the desk to ask for Detective Peter Linwood, indicating he had a message for him.

"Day off today," the desk sergeant told him. "You can leave a message if you like. Or, he'll be on duty tomorrow, but maybe in or out, depends."

"That's okay, I'll catch him another time."

"Wanna leave your name, where he can reach you?" the desk sergeant asked.

The visitor was a tall, athletic-looking man with a shaved head who reminded the sergeant of a professional basketball player. He exuded an air of confidence, of quick alertness, and when the officer tried to elicit more information, he waved his hand and left the area.

The sergeant made a note of the visitor and placed it in Peter's mail slot.

A few weeks later, Sherissa and Zeus returned to her condo despite the protests of her parents that she remain at their home a little longer.

"I've got to be on my own," she insisted. "It's not that I don't appreciate your help, Mom and Dad, but it's time for me to get going. The doctor says I'm weeks ahead in my therapy."

"But you know what a scare we've all had," her mother said, pleading for her daughter to stay.

"All the more reason to get on with our lives," she said to her mother. "Have to do it or we'll be really fearful for life, and I can't live like that, Mother."

Sherissa had an added agenda for leaving her

parents' safe haven, one that she admitted only to herself. She knew that her feelings for Peter were reaching a critical stage way beyond friendship. Unencumbered by her parents hovering over her, she needed to be on her own to think and to probe her true feelings toward the detective. She'd made a mistake with Jack Davona. She wanted to be sure this time.

She had planned a simple meal for their dinner that evening. She and Peter had eaten out at many of the areas finest restaurants and they had discovered a shared love for seafood.

At the local supermarket she bought shiitaki mushrooms stuffed with shrimp for appetizers, a scallop casserole with tartar sauce, and a crisp salad of mixed greens. All she had to do was mix the salad with slices of avocado and drizzle a light, tangy dressing over it prior to serving. At the bakery she bought small, light crescent rolls which she planned to serve warm with sweet butter.

Aware of Peter's desire to keep fit, she decided to serve a fresh fruit cup for dessert that she prepared herself. She diced apples, pears, bananas, grapefruit, and oranges and mixed them together. She added fresh orange juice and stirred all the fruit and juice in a crystal bowl which she placed covered with plastic in the refrigerator. Just before serving she planned to sprinkle shredded coconut on her ambrosia, as she called it. She bought wafer thin ginger cookies to serve with it.

She checked the fridge. The wine she planned to serve was chilling and she hoped she had made the right selections with the zinfandel and the chardonnay.

In her living room, in front of a large window, was a gate-leg table that remained folded most of the time. It usually held books, current magazines, and a small lamp. Sherissa moved everything from the table, opened the gate-legs to form a small round table that made an intimate table setting for two.

In keeping with her Chinese motif, she placed red bamboo placemats on the table, thinking red is the Chinese color for good luck. *What will it bring me?* she wondered.

She placed red and gold Chinese patterned dishes on the mats and decided that her crystal wine glasses would do. She put the lamp in the center of the table and was pleased with the soft glow it offered.

The realization that she had unexpected powerful and intense feelings for Peter almost overwhelmed her. Probably, she thought, because he showed such caring, such concern for her welfare that made her feel safe and secure. She had not expected to feel this way. And she wondered, could she, should she trust this feeling? Were these true feelings of love or was it just a reaction to what they had been through together?

She looked at the table. It was ready. She checked the food and decided she had everything the way she wanted. She had only to turn on the oven to heat things up when Peter arrived.

She went into her bathroom and took a relaxing shower, delighted that she no longer wore a cast and could indulge her whole body to the soothing balm and soft caress of the welcome, soothing warm water. Unbidden, her thoughts turned to Peter. Somehow she knew tonight her life was about to change.

Thirty-One

Peter's gift to Sherissa that night was a beautifully potted plant set in a decorative brass vase.

"Peter! What a gorgeous cyclamen. I love this rose tint. My favorite color."

"I wanted you to have something you could keep for awhile. I know they say it's a delicate flower, but then I think of you as delicate." He kissed her on the cheek, and slightly flustered, she hurried over to place the gift on her coffee table, aware that the crisp clean scent of his aftershave lotion was heightening her emotions. And, she realized, the evening had just started.

Walking behind her into the living room, Peter remarked, "Your table looks great."

She invited him to have a seat on the sofa and she went into the kitchen to return with a silver tray. On it were two glasses of chilled wine and a plate with the shrimp-stuffed mushrooms. She handed him a napkin and motioned for him to help himself, which he did.

"These are wonderful," he said as he savored the appetizer. "Did you make these?"

She laughed in response, a sound he was pleased to hear after all the trauma she'd endured. "Do elephants have wings? No, Peter, as long as the supermarket has a deli, I'm relieved of kitchen duty."

"Well, I for one am happy that you still have a sense of humor after all you've been through."

"You know, Peter," she said and a sobering look came over her face.

"Know what?" he asked.

"I found out something about myself."

"Really?"

"Yes. My parents and my twin brother have always been very, very protective of me. Something I've always resented, somehow, and I've always rebelled against their attempts to make decisions for me. But this experience, the whole thing, has taught me that when I was up against it, I *could* come through somehow."

"And, *girl,*" he offered, "did you *ever* come through!"

"Of course I can't take all the credit. Couldn't have done it with your help. You're my hero!"

"Maybe we ought to thank the cell phone company," Peter suggested. "We wouldn't have been successful without that equipment."

Sherissa cleared the table, went into the kitchen and returned with the hot casserole and the salad.

"Ummm. Looks good," Peter told her.

"Thanks. Hope you like it."

"I'm sure I will," he said as she served him. "So, you found out that you had strengths you didn't know you had. Thank God you did, because let me tell you, Sheri, being a policeman, I was scared to death of what could happen to you. And I blamed myself for not protecting you."

"My dad told me he had planned to pay the ransom."

"Right. He was, and we had a hidden tracking device

in the briefcase with the money so when the drop was made, it would lead us to your kidnappers."

"I understand even the FBI was called in."

"They were. It's a federal crime, you know, kidnapping."

"I was sure glad that you and the lieutenant were able to understand my messages. You were my only hope."

"Honey, you're a smart, clever girl and got through to us just fine."

She shook her head. "Peter, you don't know how scared I was. Never been so scared in my life!"

He saw the memory of her dreadful experience cloud her eyes and he reached across the table to take her hand and give it a gentle squeeze.

"It's behind us now, Sheri, and now it's time to move forward with your life and," he squeezed her hand again to emphasize his intentions, "if you'll let me, I'd like to be a part of your life."

She smiled at him. "You've certainly been a big part so far, Peter," she said. Then she hedged a bit with her next statement. "Oh, before I forget, my station manager, Mr. Osgood, told me that I've been invited to appear on national television. The Oprah Winfrey Show. And Jay Leno wants me, too. He's originally from around this area, you know."

"Think you'll do it?"

"Not sure. Mr. Osgood thinks it might be good publicity for the station, but I'm not certain."

"At a time like this you need to make you *own* decisions, you know," he told her, gently rubbing his fingers along her arm and hands. Her skin felt silky, warm and smooth, and he ached to hold her close. She wore a long silk skirt printed in Kente cloth stripes and a black silk sleeveless blouse with a scoop neckline that revealed her lovely throat. A thin gold chain graced her neck and the tiny gold studs in her ears only enhanced the lovely delicate shape of her head. The way her trim short hair curled around her ears enchanted him and memories of how he could have lost her boggled his mind. He searched his brain for the proper words to express his feelings. Would he find them or would his heart override his brain and force him to blurt out nonsense like an oversexed teenager? When would the proper moment come? Would it be tonight?

Together they took the dishes into the kitchen.

Sherissa explained, "I'll put them in the dishwasher for now and run them through the cycle later. All I need to do now is wash and dry the wine glasses."

"Okay," Peter said, "you wash and I'll dry." It felt natural to him to be standing so close to her, and inwardly he was delighted with the intense intimate feeling.

At that moment Zeus walked in from Sherissa's bedroom where he had been sleeping and peered into his bowl.

"Zeus, my man, how are you? Glad to be back home, I know." Peter said to the cat.

He bent down to run his hand along the cat's silky smooth black fur and the cat purred contentedly.

"He likes you, Peter."

"And I like him. I had a cat and a dog when I was a kid. When you learn to love animals, all God's creatures, you learn to be patient."

"And patience is something you need in police work, I'm sure."

"I've discovered that, all right. My lieutenant, John Williams, has taught me that."

They left the kitchen to Zeus, who was still

enjoying his food. Peter's heartbeat struggled to maintain a steady pace as they returned to the living room. He felt he needed to make conversation to fill the sudden vacuum that came now that the meal was finished.

"So," he ventured, "have you decided to return to work full-time?"

"Just as soon as my doctor gives me the green light."

"You do seem to be walking well. No trouble with your ankle?"

"No," and she grinned at him like a mischievous child. "but I can sure tell you when it's going to rain. Something about the atmospheric pressure that makes broken bones ache."

He felt an ache, too. An ache that only loving the lovely Sherissa could ease. The ache that had started the very day he met her to ask questions about the hit and run accident. That day that he had appeared belligerent and antagonistic, as dense and as stupid as a wet-behind-the-ears rookie. Did she see him differently now? He surely hoped so.

Zeus walked in at that moment and stretched himself, his sleek muscles rippling in the soft light from the table lamp.

"Watch this," Sherissa whispered.

As Peter and Sherissa sat quietly on the sofa, they watched as the cat walked the perimeter of the room as if sniffing and tracking an unwanted intruder. He jumped to the window sill, continued to sniff until satisfied that all was as it should be. He jumped to the floor, and then with a satisfied meow, strolled into the bedroom.

"He's done that house-checking routine ever since he was a kitten," Sherissa explained.

"Man after my own heart. Wants to make certain *his*

territory is secure." Peter stood up. "I'd better leave before Zeus decides to throw me out."

"He does act like he's the boss, doesn't he, but you don't have to leave. Would you like some coffee before you go? Not that you've had that much to drink."

"Thanks, but no thanks, Sheri. It was a lovely meal."

As they walked toward her front door, Peter was trying to prepare himself to say good night to the only woman he wanted in his life. Would the right words come to him? Would she understand their meaning?

At the door he hesitated for a brief moment, then he placed both hands on her shoulders. She responded to the gesture by stepping into his embrace. When his lips touched hers, soft, willing, and receptive, he thrilled to taste, at last, the sweet unmistakable passion that she offered. Then, unexpectedly, she tore her mouth away from his, her head between his shoulder and neck, she clung to him and began to sob uncontrollably.

Stunned by her reaction, Peter could only hold her closer. "Oh, baby, don't cry. It's all over now. You're safe. I'll never let anyone hurt you again. Never, I swear! Don't cry, please."

It seemed to him as if all the tormenting experiences Sherissa had endured had suddenly overwhelmed her and the strong facade she'd tried to maintain had crumbled.

Concerned, Peter could feel the quivering tremors that rippled through her delicate frame as she continued to sob and cling to him. She was almost hysterical, her gasping sounds, hiccoughs, and tears tore at Peter.

"Oh, Peter, hold me, please hold me," she begged. Her voice broke then and she looked at him with tear-stained eyes.

"Never thought, never . . . ever that I'd be safe. Oh, I . . . I was so scared I was going to be killed!"

He kissed her because he couldn't help himself and he wanted her to end the litany of fear which distressed her. His heart broke for her and one thing he was positive about, he couldn't leave her. Not now, not tonight.

Thirty-Two

Gently, Peter walked Sherissa back to the living room. He sat her down on the sofa, then went into the bathroom. He returned with a box of tissues he found and a face cloth wrung out with warm water.

He handed her a tissue to wipe her tears away and blow her nose. Then with a delicate touch he wiped her face with the soft warm cloth.

She gave him a shy smile. "Sorry I made such a scene, Peter. Don't know what happened."

"It just all came down on you, what you've been through, that's all. It's very understandable." Then he looked directly into her eyes. "I'm not leaving you alone tonight."

Her eyes widened at what he'd just said.

"You're not?"

"I'm bunking right here on the couch. Come morning, we'll see how things are."

"But . . . but you don't have to stay. What about your work . . . your job?"

"Have the weekend off, report back Monday morning. So all I need is a pillow and a blanket and I'll be fine right here." He patted the sofa.

Tears flooded her eyes again.

"Thanks, Peter."

She knew his strength, his support, and his

thoughtful kindness was what she needed in her life. No, it was more than that. She needed *him,* wanted *him* as much as her very next heartbeat. She wanted him to stay with her tonight and every night for the rest of her life.

She wiped the tears from her eyes with her knuckles to give him a weak smile.

"If you insist."

"I do."

When she went into the bathroom she was upset when she saw her reflection in the mirror. Gone was the up-and-coming professional woman. Instead she saw a sober, clean-faced anxious young woman. Which one did Peter see?

She took sheets and an extra pillow from the linen closet and then, remembering that her twin Todd had left a pair of pajamas the last time he visited, she added them to the linen pile. Peter was not as tall as her brother, but he'd have to make do somehow. She was glad he was staying the night. She wanted him to be near her. Six months ago she would have scoffed at the idea. But now all that had changed. Six months ago her life hadn't been threatened, nor had she dreamed of falling in love with a police detective named Peter Linwood.

"There's a new toothbrush for you on the bathroom counter and a disposable razor if you want to use it," she explained. "My twin is often apt to bring overnight guests, so I try to keep extras around."

"Thanks very much. I'll be fine." He stood there holding the folded blanket and pillow, wishing that instead the teary-eyed woman he loved was there in his arms. But he knew she was vulnerable after her sudden reaction to her ordeal. He had heard of such responses to untoward events.

Peter's intention was to be supportive, so he said, "You go ahead, try to relax and get some rest and remember, I'll be here if you need me. Good night now. Sleep well."

"G-good night, and thanks," Sherissa said. She went into her bedroom and Peter heard the door close.

He went into the bathroom and changed into the pajamas Sherissa had given him. They did not fit too badly. The couch in the living room was another matter. By removing the three cushions at the back he had a little more room, but as he wrapped the blanket around himself, he wondered if he would get any sleep.

He did fall asleep, but woke suddenly, and for a brief moment, unsure of his surroundings. Then he remembered where he was. He checked his watch. Almost three. He lay for a moment, the blanket covering more of the floor than his body. Then he heard furtive noises. They seemed to be coming from the kitchen. He got up to investigate.

"Sheri, what's wrong?"

"Didn't mean to disturb you, Peter. Couldn't sleep." He saw that she had placed a small sauce pan and a bottle of milk on the kitchen counter.

"Do you have any brandy? Sometimes a little bit in the milk will help."

She rummaged about in one of the lower cabinets and found some brandy.

"This might be kinda old."

"All the better."

She sniffled as she poured the warm milk into a mug.

"I'm not cryin' because I'm scared. I'm just mad at myself for being so shook up. Don't like the feeling, not at all!"

"You have every right to feel shaky," he tried to reassure her.

"I hate being so . . . so wishy-washy. It's not me!"

"But, Sheri, like I said, it's normal, like the aftershocks of an earthquake. It takes a while for your world to settle down . . . to return to even keel again. Come here," he knew he looked strange with the blanket draped Indian fashion around his shoulders in lieu of a bathrobe, but he opened the blanket and pulled her in close. She still held the mug of warm milk in her hand. He took her back to the living room and they sat down on the sofa.

Sherissa took a few sips of her brandy-flavored milk, finally placing the cup back on the table. She relaxed a bit and allowed Peter to hold her. She yielded to her uneasy desire and surrendered to the feelings that she had held in abeyance for so long. Peter's masculine hard body was what she needed. Tears still glistened in her eyes as she looked up at him. He touched her face as if she were a delicate doll and he was afraid that his fingers would bruise her. He made his fingers light and gentle as he caressed her tenderly. Her skin was soft and pliant to his touch.

He kissed the glistening teardrops from her closed eyes, then he tilted her chin and lowered his lips to hers. She responded to his gesture by parting her lips beneath his so that his tongue could explore the brandy-flavored sweetness inside.

Sherissa moaned as whirls of unbridled delight coursed through her body. She thought she would go mad. She wanted desperately to feel his skin, to touch him everywhere. She had never known such mad desire.

Peter's mouth was everywhere, at her eyes, her earlobes, the nape of her neck, her throat, and then he pulled her nightgown down over her shoulders to stare in the soft light at her glorious breasts. He bent his head to take one precious aroused orb in his mouth while with his fingers he plundered the other.

Sherissa cried out as delicate ripples of sweet passion savaged her body. Peter threw off the blanket, picked Sherissa up in his arms and took her into the bedroom. He never saw Zeus leave, and he closed the door with his foot.

Gently he deposited Sherissa on the bed, then he quickly shed his clothing. Her eyes widened when she saw him and realized that the magic in the room had been created by the two of them. She pulled her nightgown down to her feet and kicked it to the floor, then she raised her arms to Peter.

Peter lay beside her, pulling her to him.

"I love you, Sherissa Holland. Have since the day I first laid eyes on you." He ran his fingers down along her thighs, caressed her with warm, soft, yet strong fingers as Sherissa responded with squirming movements and breathless pleas of her own. The delicious torment she felt could be eased only by Peter and she knew it. She reached beneath her pillow to hand him a silver packet.

He accepted the gift of trust, his eyes never leaving hers. What she saw reflected in them assured her that this man wanted her. Wanted her to be safe, protected, and loved. Peter *was* the right one, the one she loved, would always love.

She felt as if she would die if the yearning, longing feelings that swept over her whole tingling body were not appeased.

A hoarse moan slipped through her lips.

"Peter! Please, love me! Love me, now!" she begged.

Moving over her quickly, sheathed and eager, he responded to her plea. He held her face with both hands to kiss her. Her fervent responses matched his and when their bodies fused into an indescribable intimacy, breathless and spent, they clung to each other and slept.

Thirty-Three

Sergeant Palmer found Peter at his desk.

"Hey," he asked him, "did you ever get that message I left in your box?"

"Yeah, thanks, Sarge, I did. But I wasn't expecting anyone to come to the station. And you said the guy didn't leave his name or a message?"

"Right. Said he'd be back maybe later. I thought he might be one of your street informers. He looked the type, you know, bold, arrogant, sure of himself."

"Wouldn't tell you why he was looking for me?"

"No, but anyway," Peter waved the officer to the chair next to his desk and Sergeant Palmer sat down to continue his story, "like I said, there was something about him that bothered me. I had a real slow night at the desk so I thought I'd go over some mug shots . . . see if I could identify him. I remembered that you and the lieutenant have been working on this case together, figured maybe this might lead to something. And sure enough, I spotted him."

"You did? Man, you're something else with that photographic memory you've got."

"Yeah, right, and this time it panned out. Lucky 'Doc' Reynolds. Remember him?"

"I sure do." Peter's eyes widened at the memory of the cohort that A.B. Hodges had summoned from the

Caribbean to take care of any of his victim's medical problems. Said to have remained in medical school long enough to learn about abortions and other illegal surgical procedures. He was reported to have a born surgeon's hands.

"He's the one the Las Vegas police are lookin' for in that airplane murder."

Sergeant Palmer agreed. "There was just something about him. Although he looked as if he could use some money, there was a defiant, almost combatant attitude . . ."

"I know the look," Peter said, "The 'I dare you, come and git me' look."

"What have the Nevada police come up with?"

"For starters," Peter told him, "they went over the whole plane with a fine-toothed comb, so to speak. They removed the seats not only where the perp and the victim sat, but the two seats ahead and the two seats behind. All six were sent to the forensics lab. They found the empty syringe wedged down the seat cushions and they got a real good thumb print on one of the in-flight magazine covers."

"Well," Sergeant Palmer said, "with the sheet we've got on him, there's enough to bring him in. I'm sure there's a positive link between him and Gus Hodges. Talk it over with your partner, why don't you? Let me know if I can be of further help."

"Thanks for what you've already done. It's goin' to help tie up loose ends, I think, and bring closure."

Peter's thoughts were whirling about with the mention of Gus Hodges. Since he and Sherissa had decided to get married, he was most anxious that no cloud such as the machinations of the amoral, criminal Augustus Bell Hodges interfere with their lives.

However, acknowledging the vengeful tentacles of

Hodges, Peter could believe that the criminal would be out to get anyone who had messed with his plans, including the police. He had to let his partner know about this latest development at once.

Sergeant Palmer placed his hands on his knees, prepared to stand up. When he did so, almost as an afterthought, he said, "Peter, wouldn't surprise me to find out that Hodges sent that goon here to make trouble for you and the lieutenant."

"I'm goin' to fill him in right away, Sarge, and get Las Vegas to fax a copy of the thumb print, see if it matches what we've got on file. And, Sarge, thanks again."

The two shook hands. "No problem. You know once I see a face and can't name the person, it drives me nuts 'til I can figure it out."

"Great talent to have. Glad you're on our side. Thanks again."

"Anytime. Well, I'm off. Have a good day and watch your back. It's a jungle out there."

Peter watched the older, seasoned officer leave. He knew exactly what the man meant. He hoped by tying up this loose end about the murder of Tyree Embrey the whole case could be resolved. And Sergeant Palmer had inferred that both he and the lieutenant could be the target of Hodges's wrath, even though he was already in custody, having been found guilty of money laundering. However, even in a federal prison he was still able to manipulate his hirelings.

As soon as John Williams arrived that morning and took his seat at his desk across from Peter, Peter began to brief him on the new information he'd just received from the desk sergeant.

The lieutenant listened carefully, nodding his head in agreement as Peter finished.

"Not surprised that Hodges would send someone to try to take us out. He's a vindictive, vicious son of a bitch who uses fear tactics to manipulate his enemies and to keep his soldiers in line. See, if he could wipe us out, intimidate the police, it would give him more power over his flunkies. Oh, yes, they admire and respect someone who doesn't seem to fear the police."

"I understand that mentality, John. So what's our next step?"

"Hmmm. If the thumb print Las Vegas has matches what we have in our files here on Reynolds, we'll put out an APB on him and have him picked up. The state of Nevada may want us to extradite him out there since the murder probably took place there, but then since the murder may have taken place in flight, it may come under federal jurisdiction. But if he's around here in Boston, we'll get him."

"I've heard that he follows the horses. Probably be over at Suffolk Downs today." Peter looked at his watch. "First race starts at one-thirty. Maybe there now, checking things out before the actual races begin."

"We'll get the all-points bulletin out. When and if we nab him, all the loose ends of this case should be tied up. Listen to this. Got word yesterday that Hodges has been diagnosed with a terminal illness."

"He still in prison?" Peter asked.

"Prison hospital with around-the-clock care. You know he's been convicted of capital murder which can carry a death penalty," the lieutenant said. Then he added, "May beat that sentence, however. They say he has cancer and doesn't have much time left."

Peter shook his head at this latest revelation. "He's certainly been the master plotter behind all of these crimes. But what about Jack Davona?"

"He and his high-priced lawyer cut a deal with the

district attorney. Going to pay a hefty fine. Claimed not to have known he was dealing with Hodges' drug-money–laundering business. Word is that he's relocating in San Francisco. Had to sell the publishing company here, but plans to start up a franchise for the company out west. Quite a comedown, I'd say." The lieutenant raised his hand high in the air, then brought it down to rest on his desk. "From head honcho to employee: How the mighty can fall."

Peter remained silent, thinking about all the events of the past weeks and his involvement because he was a police detective. But, out of the untoward circumstances, he had been blessed to receive a treasure beyond price. John Williams had mentioned it more than once, there's nothing to equal the love and support of a good woman, and now he, Peter Linwood, could honestly attest to that fact.

Today, life was great, the future was bright, and no matter what happened from here on out, loving Sherissa and being loved by her was almost more than he had hoped for in this life.

He sighed deeply and audibly, causing John to take a sharp look at him.

"You all right?"

Abruptly, Peter slapped both hands on the arm rests of his chair and stood up. He walked over to John's side of the desk, and with a wide grin thrust out his hand. Willingly, John grasped Peter's hand and the two shook hands.

"Never felt better, John. Never! But I'd like to ask you to do a favor for me."

"Sure, anytime. What can I do for you?"

"We've been through a lot together working on these cases. You've been supportive of me, and God knows I sure had a lot to learn and," he hesitated for a moment before adding, "Sherissa Holland and I are getting married and what I want to know is . . . will you be my best man?"

"Good God, son, the honor is mine!" John grasped Peter's hand again and shook it heartily. "It will be a privilege and a pleasure to stand beside my partner."

He walked over to the coffee pot and poured a steaming hot mug for each of them. He raised his cup to Peter.

"To everlasting happiness and wedded bliss."

"Thank you, sir," Peter answered. "It means a great deal to me for you to do this."

"As I said, the pleasure is mine. Let's go on over to The Good Egg and have some lunch before it gets too crowded."

They put on their jackets and walked down the stairs to the lieutenant's car. Each man was aware that before long they could be racing down these same stairs on their way to investigate another homicide.

As he jumped into the passenger seat, fastened his seat belt, Peter voiced the thoughts going through his mind at that moment.

"You know something, John?"

"No, what?"

"I'm just thinking, we're in a noble profession, you and I, trying to bring justice to victims who have lost the most valuable thing they had . . . their lives."

"That's what makes it noble, son," his partner said as he checked the side mirror for oncoming traffic before moving into the street.

"We make it right for those who can't help themselves by making the evildoers pay for their crimes. And there's more to it. It's laws and rules of evidence that keeps us living in a civil society. There'll always be a criminal element, people like Hodges and his kind."

Peter nodded his head thoughtfully as he listened to John.

"You know, when I was growin' up, my grandmother used to say wicked, evil type people were bad to the bone. She said they were wicked through and through, with no truth or goodness in them."

"She was right, my man. So, to keep our world a civil, safe place, we have to practice our noble profession each and every day. Now, on to The Good Egg so you can brief me on your wedding and what my duties will be as your best man."

Thirty-Four

The wedding took place in the elegant floral setting provided by the Holland's well-designed backyard. An altar-like trellis decorated with roses, ivy, and baby's breath had been set up at the far end of the garden, reached by a flagstone foot path. A profusion of freshly cut summer flower arrangements in large white urns were everywhere, from lining the bridal path, to the end of each row of glistening white chairs for the two hundred invited guests. A white tent for the wedding reception had been placed near the patio for the convenience of the caterers, and from that location a string quartet provided the bridal music.

With the lieutenant as his best man standing beside him at the altar, and Sherissa's brother, Todd, and Elijah, the Celtics player as ushers, Peter stood at the flower-draped altar, waiting for his bride.

John's daughter, Kendra, had been almost delirious with excitement at being selected by Sherissa as a junior bridesmaid. She looked quite grown up in her pink, off-the-shoulder-gown. Her hair done in braids, coronet style. She wore a tiara of pink rosebuds. Her father nudged Peter with his elbow as his only child walked toward them.

"My pride and joy," he whispered.

Peter nodded, too emotional at that moment to reply.

Sherissa's friend, Elise, came next as maid of honor, looking serene and lovely in rose silk. After she reached the altar, the music changed to the wedding march and everyone stood, all eyes on the bride.

John had to place a restraining arm on Peter to keep him from rushing to Sherissa before she reached the altar.

"Easy, son, easy," he whispered softly. "Everything is okay, relax."

Later that day Peter told Sherissa that he was so excited when he saw her coming toward him he was unaware of anyone else. "All I could see was you, my beloved, my bride, who would spend the rest of her life with me! Sheri, honey, you were the most beautiful woman I'd ever seen. I thought what a lucky man I am!"

About four that afternoon a plainclothes policeman asked to speak to Lieutenant Williams. The two men moved to the far corner of the fence in the yard and conversed quietly near the boxwood hedge. After a few moments of conversation, the policeman left and John Williams went in search of the bridegroom.

Mr. Holland directed him.

"Peter's gone upstairs to change, lieutenant. Think they'll be leaving for their honeymoon in an hour or so."

"Thanks, Mr. Holland, only take a moment of his time."

"Not bad news, I hope."

"Oh, no, sir, not at all," John hastened to reassure Peter's new father-in-law.

"Hey, my man!" he greeted Peter when he found him. "Just about set to go?"

"Sure am. And again, John, thanks for standing by me. Meant a lot to me to have you in my corner."

John waved his hand in a gesture of dismissal, saying, "The pleasure was all mine, you know that. Look, I know you're short of time, but have something to tell you that I think you'll want to know."

"What's that?" Peter questioned.

"Word came last night that Hodges died at the prison hospital, and a few minutes ago one of my men came by to tell me that Doc Reynolds has been picked up and is in police custody."

"I don't believe it," Peter said. "He's in custody?"

"Yep, awaiting extradition to the state of Nevada."

"So that means all the loose ends are tied up."

"That's what it means, Peter. This case is behind us now, thanks to your good work."

"My good work, sir? I only followed your lead, and I learned a lot in the process."

"Okay," the lieutenant slapped Peter on the back, then took his hand in a vigorous warm handshake, "'go forth and multiply', as the Good Book says."

"Is that an order?" Peter asked with a broad grin.

"It surely is. That's an order!" the lieutenant laughed.

"Yes, sir!" Peter saluted and bounded down the stairs to find his wife.

As he went down the stairs, he thought how lucky he was to have the love of a good woman like Sherissa. His mind was filled with hope and he prayed that the vows they had taken just a short while ago would never change.

His grandparents were waiting at the foot of the stairs to say goodbye to him. His grandmother looked serene and elegant in a gray silk dress with pearls at her neck. Her eyes filled with tears as she hugged him, seemingly reluctant to let him go.

"She's already in your car, waitin' on you, son," she whispered in his ear.

His grandfather grabbed him in a tight bear hug. "God go with you, son. Have a happy and fruitful life. Now," he gave him a slight push, "don't keep your wife waitin'!"

"That an order, Gramps?" Peter asked, a wide grin on his face.

His grandfather took a step back, clicked his heels together and saluted smartly.

"That's an order, Sarge!"

Peter returned the salute, ran to the car, and got into the driver's seat beside a waiting Sherissa. He kissed her, started the motor, and as they waved good-bye to the wedding guests, he told her, "I've got orders."

"What do you mean, *orders*? Aren't we going on our honeymoon?" she frowned at him. Even more puzzled when Peter laughed.

"The first order from the lieutenant was to go forth and multiply, and the second order from Gramps was not to keep you waiting. So I aim to follow them both! Look out world, here come the Linwoods! Are you ready, my lovely wife?"

"Ready and willing," she told him.

Dear Readers:

It has been my distinct pleasure to write books for you such as BAD TO THE BONE. Your interest and support have given me the incentive to try to write books that will please you. I am grateful for the opportunity to do so.

Sincerely,
Mildred Riley
Whitman, Massachusetts

ABOUT THE AUTHOR

Mildred Riley is a native of Connecticut. She makes her home in Whitman, Massachusetts.

More Sizzling Romances From
Carmen Green

More Arabesque Romances by
Monica Jackson

MORE ROMANCE FROM
ANGELA WINTERS

__**A FOREVER PASSION**
   1-58314-077-8 $5.99US/$7.99CAN

__**ISLAND PROMISE**
   0-7860-0574-2 $5.99US/$7.99CAN

__**SUDDEN LOVE**
   1-58314-023-9 $4.99US/$6.50CAN

__**KNOW BY HEART**
   1-58314-215-0 $5.99US/$7.99CAN

__**THE BUSINESS OF LOVE**
   1-58314-150-2 $5.99US/$7.99CAN

__**ONLY YOU**
   0-7860-0352-9 $4.99US/$6.50CAN

Call toll free **1-888-345-BOOK** to order by phone or use this coupon to order by mail.

Name_____

Address_____

City_____ State _____ Zip _____

Please send me the books I have checked above.

I am enclosing	$_____
Plus postage and handling*	$_____
Sales tax (in NY, TN, and DC)	$_____
Total amount enclosed	$_____

*Add $2.50 for the first book and $.50 for each additional book.
Send check or money order (no cash or CODs) to: **Arabesque Romances, Dept. C.O., 850 Third Avenue, 16th Floor, New York, NY 10022**
Prices and numbers subject to change without notice.
All orders subject to availability.
Visit our website at **www.arabesquebooks.com.**

More Sizzling Romance From
Leslie Esdaile